愛
經
典

閱讀經典，成為更好的自己。

親愛的
Dear_____

這是海明威
This is a precious gift

留給我們的珍貴禮物
Hemingway left for us

我把它送給你
Here I present it to you

_____

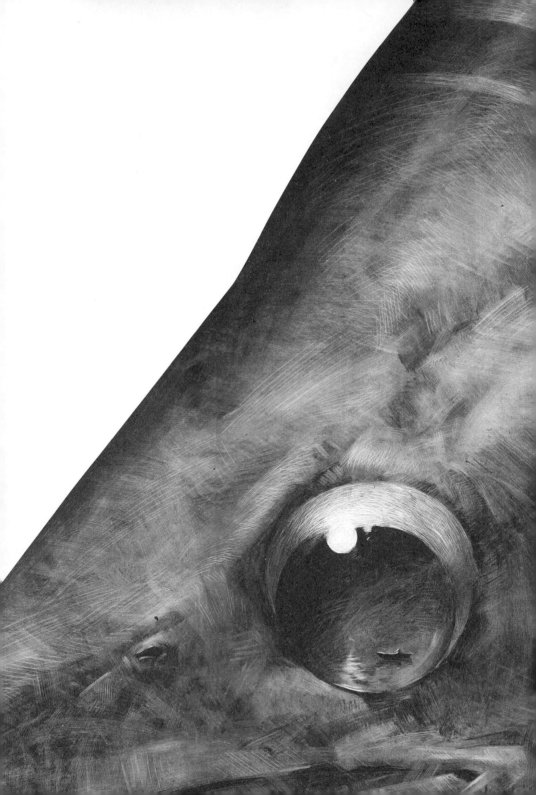

老人與海

THE OLD MAN AND THE SEA

ERNEST HEMINGWAY

歐內斯特·海明威 著 魯羊 譯

愛經典

卡爾維諾說：「『經典』即是具影響力的作品，在我們的想像中留下痕跡，並藏在潛意識中。正因『經典』有這種影響力，我們更要撥時間閱讀，接受『經典』為我們帶來的改變。」因為經典作品具有這樣無窮的魅力，時報出版公司特別引進大星文化公司的「作家榜經典文庫」，期能為臺灣的經典閱讀提供另一選擇。

作家榜經典文庫從二〇一七年起至今，已出版超過六十本，迅速累積良好口碑，不斷榮登豆瓣讀書暢銷榜。本書系的作者都經過時代淬鍊，其作品雋永，意義深遠；所選擇的譯者，多為優秀的詩人、作家，因此譯文流暢，讀來如同原創作品般通順，沒有隔閡；而且時報在臺推出時，每部作品皆以精裝裝幀，質感更佳，是讀者想要閱讀與收藏經典時的首選。

現在開始讀經典，成為更好的自己。

歐內斯特・海明威
Ernest Hemingway，1899—1961

美國歷史上最耀眼的傳奇作家，諾貝爾文學獎、普立茲獎得主。

出生於美國芝加哥的一座小鎮，和父親一樣熱愛大自然，喜歡打獵、捕魚，在森林和湖泊中露營。

高中畢業後拒上大學，十八歲就成為知名媒體記者。參加過兩次世界大戰，擔任過救護車司機，在前線被炮彈炸成重傷，差點送命。結過四次婚。著有《戰地鐘聲》、《戰地春夢》、《太陽依舊升起》、《流動的饗宴》、《我們的時代》等；一九五二年出版的《老人與海》為其巔峰之作，並以此書分別獲得諾貝爾文學獎和普立茲獎。

一九六一年，因舊傷纏身，精神憂鬱，六十二歲的海明威在家中用獵槍自盡。

作家榜推薦詞

世上有一頭豪豬，因為愛上藝術和女人而變成了海明威。

他的一生基本上是不可模仿的，他的抑鬱症不可模仿，他身體裡二二七塊彈片不可模仿，兩次飛機失事不可模仿，四次婚姻不可模仿，十三次腦震盪不可模仿，他酗酒不可模仿，他打女人不可模仿，他去古巴吸大麻不可模仿，他到非洲獵殺獅子不可模仿，他十六歲那年打架差點打瞎眼睛不可模仿，他六十二歲那年朝自己的喉嚨開槍最終把腦袋打開花萬萬不可模仿。

但他的一些好習慣廣受世人的頌揚：每天六點起床；聽莫札特；看哥雅的油畫；將小說的最後一頁修改三十九遍；每年讀一次莎士比亞的詩篇。

為了作品簡潔，他餓著肚子寫、單腳踮著地寫、在寒冬中故意只穿一件單衣凍得瑟瑟發抖寫。這些變態的寫作讓他的小說裡幾乎找不出一句廢話。

他活著，是一個傳奇，被偉大的馬奎斯膜拜；他的死，是一面喪旗，展開巨大的陰影，籠罩了海明威家族數十年，成為一個魔咒，讓美國人談虎色變。

如果沒有海明威，美國文學會怎麼樣？這不堪設想。但可以設想的是，看過《老人與海》的，是一種人；沒看過《老人與海》的，是另一種人。

有關《老人與海》，再也沒有比他的老對手福克納的說法更精妙了：那個老人，一定要逮住那條魚然後又失去他；那條魚，一定要被逮住然後又消失；那些鯊魚，一定要把魚從老人的手裡奪走；是他創造出這一切、愛這一切，又憐憫這一切。這一次，他找到了上帝。

作為兩個被上帝選擇的寵兒，他與福克納都是美國佬，他與福克納卻老死不相往來，他與福克納都得到瑞典文學院的青睞，他與福克納的文字都給這個宇宙帶來不朽的光輝。

究竟，什麼樣的文字堪稱不朽？我們需要怎樣的慎重和純潔？

所有的原則自天而降：那就是你必須相信魔法、相信美、相信那些在百萬個鑽石中總結我們的人、相信此刻你手捧的魯羊先生的譯本，就是「不朽」這個璀璨的詞語給出的最好的佐證。

二〇一六年十一月二十三日於作家榜

何三坡

9

── 目次 ──

老人與海

THE OLD MAN
AND THE SEA

他是個老人，孑然一身，駕著小船，在墨西哥灣流中釣魚，如今已是連續八十四天一無所獲了。最初的四十天裡，有個男孩跟隨他出海，但在整整四十天沒有釣到魚之後，男孩的父母對他說，這老人現在絕對是一條翻不了身的死鹹魚，倒楣透頂。在他們的安排下，男孩跟了另一條船，頭一個星期那條船就弄到三條好魚。老人的小船每天回來時都空空如也，男孩看見，心裡難過，每次都走下海灘，幫著老人搬捲好的魚線，搬拖鉤和魚叉，還有捲在桅杆上的船帆。那船帆用麵粉口袋打著許多補丁，捲攏著，像一面永遠失敗的旗幟。

老人消瘦而憔悴，頸後布滿深深的皺紋。熱帶海洋上太陽反光造成的良性皮膚癌在他面頰上留下棕色斑點。那些斑點順著面部兩側，一直延伸下去。他的雙手布滿很深的褶形傷疤，那是用魚線拖曳大魚時留下的，然而所有的傷疤，沒有一處是新的，這些傷疤都很陳舊，如同無魚的沙漠裡，那些遭到侵蝕的痕跡。

他所有的一切都是蒼老的，只有那雙眼睛除外。他的眼睛藍得像海水，歡快而不屈服。

「聖地牙哥，」他們離開小船停靠處並向岸上走去時，男孩對他說，「我又可以和你一起出海了。我們有了點錢。」

老人教男孩釣魚，男孩喜歡他。

「不，」老人說，「你跟了一條幸運的船，就跟著他們吧。」

「可是你別忘記，你曾經八十七天沒有釣到魚，然後我們一起連續三個星期每天都釣到了大魚。」

「我沒忘記，」老人說，「我知道你離開我，不是因為對我沒信心。」

「是爸爸讓我離開的。我是孩子，所以我要聽他的。」

「我知道，」老人說，「這很正常。」

「他不太有信心。」

「是啊，」老人說，「可是我們有，不是嗎？」

「當然，」男孩說。

「我可以請你在露臺酒吧喝杯啤酒嗎？然後我們再把東西拿回家。」

「好得很，」老人說，「一個漁夫請另一個漁夫。」

他們坐在露臺酒吧，許多漁夫拿老人尋開心，而老人並不生氣。上了年紀的漁夫中，有一些看著老人，很難過，不過他們並沒有表露出來。他們只是有禮貌地談起了海流和他們放魚鉤的深度，還談起了持續的好天氣，以及他們在海上的見聞。當天有所收穫的漁夫已經回來了，並且收拾好他們的馬林魚。魚放滿了整整兩塊木板，每塊木板的每一頭由兩個人抬著，顛顛巍巍地走向魚庫。在那裡，這些魚會被裝上冷藏車，送往哈瓦那的市場。那些捕到鯊魚的人會把鯊魚送到海灣對面的鯊魚工廠，在那裡，鯊魚被吊在滑車上，肝被取走、魚翅被割掉、皮也被剝掉，然後肉被切成條狀，以備醃製。

刮東風的時候，鯊魚工廠的氣味會越過港灣飄過來；而今天，那種氣味很微弱，因為轉成了北風，又漸漸停息了，露臺酒吧那兒陽光充足，令人愉快。

「聖地牙哥。」男孩說。

他所有的一切都是蒼老的，只有那雙眼睛除外。他的眼睛藍得像海水，歡快而不屈服。

「嗯。」老人應道。他端著玻璃杯，正想起多年前的往事。

「我可以出去給你弄點明天用的沙丁魚嗎？」

「不用。去玩棒球吧。我還能划船，羅傑里奧會幫我撒網。」

「我還是想去。即使不能和你一起釣魚，我還是想給你幫點忙。」

「你已經請我喝了啤酒，」老人說，「你是一個男子漢了。」

「你第一次帶我上船的時候，我多大？」

「五歲，那天我太早把魚拖進了船艙，那條魚幾乎把小船撕成了碎片，害你差點丟了小命。你還記得嗎？」

「我記得魚尾巴砰砰拍打著，船板都給拍斷了，還有用棍子打魚的聲音。我覺得整條船都在顫抖，你用棍子啪啪打魚的聲音，就像是在砍倒一棵樹。我渾身都是甜絲絲的血腥味。」

「你當真記得那些，還是後來我跟你說過？」

「從我們一起出海到現在，所有事情我都記得。」

老人用他那雙被太陽灼傷，卻充滿自信和慈愛的眼睛看著他。

「如果你是我的孩子，我一定會帶你出去賭一把，」他說，「可是你是你父母的孩子，而且你還跟了一條幸運的船。」

「我可以去弄點沙丁魚嗎？我還知道能從哪裡弄到四個魚餌。」

「我今天還有剩下的。我把他們醃在盒子裡。」

「讓我給你弄四個新鮮的吧。」

「一個就好。」老人說。他的希望和他的自信從未消失。不過此刻，這兩點又重新煥發出來，如同一陣微風吹起。

「兩個。」男孩說。

「就兩個，」老人同意了，「你不是偷的吧？」

「我倒寧願去偷，」男孩說，「但這些是我買的。」

「謝謝你。」老人說。他心地單純，不曾去想他什麼時候變得這麼謙卑，但他知道自己的這種變化，而且他還知道，這不丟臉，也無損於真正的驕傲。

「看海流的情形，明天準是好天。」他說。

「明天你要去到哪兒？」男孩問。

「能去多遠就去多遠，等轉風向的時候再回來。我想天沒亮的時候就出海。」

「我盡量讓他到離岸遠一點的地方捕魚，」男孩說，「這樣的話，如果你釣到真正的大魚，我們好趕過來幫忙。」

「他可不想在離岸太遠的地方捕魚。」

「是啊，」男孩說，「可是我會看見一些他根本看不見的東西，比如一隻覓食的小鳥，然後讓他到離岸遠的地方去追蹤鯕鰍魚。」

「他的眼睛那麼糟糕嗎？」

「他幾乎是瞎子。」

「這就奇怪了，」老人說，「他從來沒去捕過海龜。那工作才傷眼睛呢。」

「可是你有很多年在蚊子海岸那一帶捕海龜呢，而你的眼睛很好啊。」

「我這老頭可不同尋常。」

「但是現在你還有力氣去對付一條真正的大魚嗎？」

「我覺得可以。再說我還有不少技巧呢。」

「我們把東西拿回家吧，」男孩說，「我可以帶上拋網去捕沙丁魚。」

他們從船上拿起了傢伙。老人扛起了桅杆，男孩搬起了木箱，還有拖鉤和長柄魚叉。木箱裡裝著捲好，並編得很牢的棕色魚線。放魚餌的盒子和一根木棍並排放在船尾的艙裡，那木棍是用來制伏被拖到船邊的大魚的。沒人會偷老人的東西，但是船帆和粗魚線最好還是帶回家，露水會把這些東西打溼，而且儘管他確信當地沒人會偷偷他的東西，老人還是認為把拖鉤和魚叉丟在船裡是一種不必要的誘惑。

他們沿著大路一起走到老人的小屋，從敞開的門走了進去。老人把捲著帆的桅杆靠牆放下，男孩把木箱和其他東西放在桅杆旁邊。桅杆幾乎有整個房間那麼長。小屋是用大王棕葉子堅韌的包殼建造起來的。小屋裡有一床、一桌、一椅，還有一處在泥地上燒木炭做飯的地方。在用韌性十足的大王棕葉子攤平之後、交疊壘成的棕色牆壁上，掛著一幅彩色的〈耶穌聖心圖〉和一幅〈科布萊聖母圖〉，這是他妻子的遺物。那兒曾經掛著一幅她的著色照片，但是他把它取了下來，因為他每次看到，都感到分外孤單。那照片如今放在牆角的架子上，上面蓋著他乾淨的襯衫。

「你有什麼吃的嗎？」男孩問。

「有一鍋黃米飯燉魚。你想來點嗎？」

「不了，我回家吃。需要我給你生火嗎？」

「不用。我晚點再生。也許我就吃冷飯。」

「我可以拿走拋網嗎？」

「當然。」

沒有什麼拋網，男孩還記得什麼時候他們把它賣掉的。可是他們還是每天把這虛構重演一遍。男孩還知道也沒有什麼黃米飯和魚。

「八十五是一個很吉利的數字，」老人說，「你想不想看到我帶回一條光魚肉就超過一千磅的大魚呢？」

「我拿拋網去捕沙丁魚。你要不要坐在門口曬太陽？」

「好的。我有昨天的報紙，我要看看棒球賽的消息。」

男孩不知道昨天的報紙是否是另一個虛構。可是老人從床墊下面拿出了報紙。

「佩德里科在酒吧給我的。」他解釋道。

「我一弄到沙丁魚就回來。我會把你的和我的一起冰起來，明天早上再分。等我回來，你可以跟我談談棒球賽的事。」

「洋基隊不會輸的。」

「但我怕克里夫蘭印第安人隊會贏。」

「對洋基隊有點信心，我的孩子。想想偉大的狄馬喬。」

「我怕底特律老虎和克里夫蘭印第安人這兩支隊都不好惹。」

「別這麼洩氣，要不然就連辛辛那提紅人隊和芝加哥白襪隊你都會害怕的。」

「你好好看吧，等我回來後跟我說。」

「你說我們要不要買一張尾數是八十五的彩券啊？明天是第八十五天了。」

「可以啊，」男孩說，「那你最長的八十七天的偉大紀錄又怎麼說呢？」

「這不可能發生兩次的。你能弄到尾數八十五的彩券嗎？」

「我可以訂一張。」

「一張，需要兩塊五。我們跟誰借呢？」

「不用費心。我總是能借到兩塊五的。」

「我覺得或許我也行。不過我盡量不借錢。借錢的下一步就是乞討啦。」

23

「注意保暖啊，老爹，」男孩說，「別忘了現在是九月了。」

「這可是出大魚的月分啊，」老人說，「如果是五月，人人可以做漁夫。」

「我現在去捕沙丁魚了。」男孩說。

男孩回來的時候老人在椅子裡睡著了，太陽也下山了。男孩從床上拿了一條舊軍毯，鋪在椅背上，蓋住老人的雙肩。這是一雙奇怪的肩膀，雖然很老，卻依然有力。脖頸也仍然強壯，當老人向前垂著腦袋睡覺時，頸後的皺紋也不見了。他的襯衫像他的船帆一樣，打了如此多補丁，那些補丁由於陽光照射，褪成了各種深淺不一的顏色。老人的頭十分蒼老，他閉著眼睛時，臉上毫無生氣。報紙攤在他的膝蓋上，因為手臂壓著，才不至於被晚風吹走。他光著腳。

男孩離開了，等他再次回來的時候，老人還睡著。

「醒醒，老爹。」男孩把手放在老人的一邊膝蓋上。

老人睜開眼睛，那一瞬間，他好像從非常遙遠的地方回來。然後他笑了。

「你拿了什麼來？」他問。

「晚飯，」男孩說，「我們吃晚飯吧。」

「我還不太餓。」

「快來吃吧。你不能空著肚子去釣魚啊。」

「我也不是沒這麼幹過。」老人說著站起來，拿起報紙，折疊好。然後他又開始折毯子。

「你就裹著毯子吧，」男孩說，「只要我還活著，你就不會空著肚子去釣魚。」

「那就祝你長壽，你可要照顧好自己哦，」老人說，「我們吃什麼？」

「黑豆和米飯、炸香蕉，還有些燉菜。」

這些吃的，男孩用雙層金屬飯盒裝著，從露臺酒吧帶過來。他的口袋裡還有兩副刀叉和湯匙，都用餐巾紙包得好好的。

「是誰給你這些的？」

「馬丁。那個老闆。」

「我得去謝謝他。」

「我已經謝過他，」男孩說，「你不用再去謝他了。」

「我要給他一塊大魚的肚肉，」老人說，「他不是頭一回這樣幫助我們了吧？」

25

「可不是嘛。」

「除了魚肚肉，我還得送他些別的才好。他對我們真的很關心。」

「他還送了我們兩瓶啤酒。」

「我最喜歡罐裝啤酒。」

「我知道，不過今天是瓶裝的哈土伊牌啤酒，我得把瓶子還回去。」

「你想得周到，」老人說，「我們開始吧？」

「我剛才就問過你啦，」男孩輕聲對他說，「你還沒準備好之前，我可不願意打開飯盒。」

「現在我準備好啦，」老人說，「我只不過花時間洗了洗手。」

「你能在哪兒洗呢？男孩想。村子裡有自來水的地方，從這兒沿大路走下去，還隔著兩條街那麼遠呢。我真該給他帶些水來，男孩想。還有肥皂和乾淨毛巾。我怎麼這麼粗心呢？我要想辦法再弄件襯衫，還有外套，給他過冬。還得有一雙像樣的鞋子，再加上一條毯子。」

「你弄來的燉菜真好吃。」老人說。

「跟我說說棒球賽吧。」男孩請求道。

「我跟你說過的，在美國聯盟的球隊中，洋基隊是最棒的。」老人高興地說道。

「但他們今天輸了。」男孩提醒他。

「這不算什麼。偉大的狄馬喬仍然是偉大的狄馬喬！」

「他們隊裡也還有其他人呢。」

「那當然。不過他可不是其他人。要說起另一個聯盟的球隊，在布魯克林和費城兩個裡面，我會選布魯克林。當然我也沒忘記迪克·西斯勒在老公園球場打出的那些好球。」

「那些好球真是無與倫比。他是我見過擊球最遠的人。」

「你還記得那時候他常來露臺酒吧嗎？我本想帶他一起出海釣魚，但我就是不好意思開口。我讓你去問他，可是你也不好意思。」

「我記得。我們真是錯過了大好機會。也許他會跟我們去釣魚的，那樣的話，我們一輩子都會記得這件事。」

「我很想帶上偉大的狄馬喬去釣魚，」老人說，「他們說他的父親是個打魚的，也許他當初也跟我們一樣窮，能夠理解我們。」

27

「偉大的西斯勒他爸可從來沒窮過，像我這麼大的時候，他爸都在大聯盟裡打球了。」

「我像你這麼大的時候，已經在一條開往非洲的橫帆大船上當水手了，還在傍晚時看見那些海灘上的獅子了。」

「我知道。你跟我講過。」

「那我們是談非洲還是談棒球？」

「還是談棒球吧，」男孩說，「給我說說偉大的約翰．J．麥格羅吧。」

他把 J 說成西班牙語的 Jota。

「老早以前，他有時候也會到露臺酒吧來。但是只要一喝酒，就變得脾氣暴躁、說話刻薄，很不好相處。除了棒球，他還把心思用在賽馬上。至少他口袋裡一直揣著賽馬的名單，還經常在打電話時提起那些馬的名字。」

「他是個了不起的經理，」男孩說，「我爸認為他是最了不起的。」

「那是因為他來這兒的次數最多，」老人說，「要是多羅徹每年都來，你爸又會認為他是最了不起的經理了。」

「說真的，那到底誰才是最了不起的經理呢？盧克，還是邁克．岡薩雷斯？」

「我覺得他們都差不多。」

「最好的漁夫是你。」

「不，我知道有比我更好的。」

「怎麼會！」男孩說，「好漁夫很多，有些也很了不起，可是最好的還是你。」

「謝謝，你真讓我開心。但願不會來一條太厲害的魚，讓我難以招架。要不然他就證明，我們只不過嘴上了得。」

「只要你還像你說的那樣強壯，就沒有你對付不了的魚。」

「也可能我沒有自己想的那麼強壯，」老人說，「但我知道不少竅門，而且我有決心。」

「這會兒你該上床睡覺了，明天早上你才會精力充沛。我會把這些東西送回露臺酒吧去。」

「那就晚安吧。明天早上我去叫醒你。」

「你是我的鬧鐘。」男孩說。

「歲數是我的鬧鐘，」老人說，「為什麼老年人都醒得早呢？是想擁有更長的一天嗎？」

「這我不知道，」男孩說，「我只知道年輕人睡到很晚都起不來。」

「我會記得的，」老人說，「我會準時叫醒你。」

「我不喜歡讓船主來叫醒我，那樣顯得我像個傭人。」

「我懂的。」

「睡個好覺吧，老爹。」

男孩出去了。沒有點燈，他們摸黑吃了晚飯。現在老人脫了長褲，在黑暗中上了床。他把長褲捲起來，做成一個枕頭，又在裡面塞了些報紙。子，在鋪著舊報紙的床墊上睡下。

他很快就睡著了，他夢到了自己還是個孩子時看到的非洲，他夢到了長長的金色沙灘和白色沙灘，白得刺痛你的眼睛，高高的海岬，雄偉的褐色群山。如今他每天夜裡都活在非洲海岸，在夢裡他聽見海浪呼嘯，他看見當地人的小船破浪而來。他睡著的時候，能聞到甲板上瀝青和麻絮的味道，還聞到陸地上的晨風吹來非洲的氣息。

「歲數是我的鬧鐘，」老人說，「為什麼老年人都醒得早呢？是想擁有更長的一天嗎？」

通常，當他聞到這種氣息時他就醒了，穿上衣服，去叫醒男孩。但是今夜這種氣息來得很早，他在夢裡就知道，它來得太早，於是他繼續做夢，他夢見島嶼上的白色山峰在海面冉冉升起，他夢見加那利群島的各處港灣和錨地。

他不再夢見風暴，不再夢見女人，不再夢見重大事件，不再夢見大魚，不再夢見打架，不再夢見鬥力氣，也不再夢見妻子。他現在只夢見一些地方和沙灘上的獅子。那些獅子在黃昏中像小貓一樣嬉戲，他喜愛他們如同他喜愛那男孩。他從未夢見過男孩。他就這樣醒來，透過敞開的門看了看月亮，展開長褲，穿上。他在小屋外撒了泡尿，就沿著大路往上走，去叫醒男孩。他在清晨的寒氣中打著哆嗦。不過他知道打哆嗦會讓他暖和起來，而且不久之後，他就要划船了。

男孩家的大門沒有上鎖，他推開門，光著腳，輕輕走了進去。男孩睡在頭一個房間的帆布床上，殘月的光照進來，老人能夠清清楚楚地看見他。他輕輕握住男孩的一隻腳，握著它，直到男孩醒來轉身看他。老人點點頭，男孩從床邊的椅子上拿起長褲，坐在床上，穿上了。

老人走到門外，男孩跟著他。男孩很睏，老人用手搭著他的雙肩說：「真抱歉。」

「別這麼說，」男孩說，「男人該當如此。」

他們沿路走回老人的小屋，一路上，在黑暗裡，光腳的漁夫在走動，扛著他們的桅桿。

來到老人的小屋，男孩拿起裝在籃子裡的魚線捲、魚叉和拖鉤，老人把捲著帆的桅桿扛在肩上。

「你想喝咖啡嗎？」男孩問。

「我們先把東西拿到船上，然後再喝吧。」

在一家大清早就開門招待漁夫的小館子裡，他們用舊煉乳罐子喝著咖啡。

「你睡得怎麼樣，老爹？」男孩問。這會兒他漸漸清醒了，雖然那睏勁兒很難過去。

「睡得很好，馬諾林，」老人說，「我今天覺得很有信心。」

「我也是，」男孩說，「現在我要去拿我們的沙丁魚和你的新鮮魚餌。他會自己去搬那條船上用的東西，他從來不要任何人幫他搬任何東西。」

「我和他不一樣，」老人說，「你才五歲的時候，我就讓你搬東西了。」

「我記得，」男孩說，「我馬上就回來。再喝杯咖啡吧。在這兒我們可以賒帳。」

他走開了，光腳踩在珊瑚岩上，走向存放魚餌的冰屋。

老人慢慢地喝著咖啡。這就是他一整天的食物，他知道他必須喝。好長一段時間了，吃東西對他來說成了煩心事，他從來不帶午飯。他在船頭放了一瓶水，這就是他一天所需。

現在男孩拿著裹在報紙裡的沙丁魚和兩個魚餌回來了。他們沿著小路走向小船，一路上他們能感覺到腳下的沙礫。他們抬起小船，讓船滑進海水。

「祝你好運，老爹。」

「祝你好運。」老人說。他將船槳的繩扣套在槳座的栓釘上，他身子前傾，頂著船槳在海水中的阻力，在黑暗中，他將小船划出了港灣。在別處的海灘上，有別的船在出海，老人看不見那些船，因為現在月亮已經下山了，他只能聽到船槳入水和划水的聲音。

偶爾也有人在船上說話。但是多數的小船都是安靜的，只傳來船槳入水的動靜。一出港口，那些船就四散開去，每一條船都駛向他們認為有魚的地方。

老人知道他要去很遠的地方，他已經把陸地的氣息拋在身後，將小船駛進清晨大海純淨的氣息中。當他划到一片水域時，他看到磷光閃現，那是水中的馬尾藻，那片水域，漁夫都叫它「大井」，那兒的水深突然達到七百英尋。水流衝擊海底陡峭的岩壁所形成的漩渦，使各種各樣的魚兒在那兒聚集。那兒有大群的海蝦和可作魚餌的小魚，那些成群結隊地生活在水底極深洞穴裡的魷魚，有時在夜間會浮到靠近海面的地方，而在那裡出沒的較大的魚類會把他們當作食物。

黑暗中，老人能感受到早晨的臨近。他划船的時候，能聽到飛魚脫離水面時震顫的聲音，還有他們在黑暗中高飛時，堅硬的鰭翅所發出的噝噝聲。他非常喜愛飛魚。飛魚是他在海上最重要的朋友。他為鳥兒感到難過，尤其是那些小巧柔弱的黑色燕鷗，他們一直飛、一直尋找，卻幾乎什麼也找不到。他認為，鳥兒的日子比我們更艱難。也許猛禽和強壯的大鳥除外。既然大海有時如此殘酷，為什麼像海燕那樣的鳥兒卻生來如此柔弱而精巧呢？大海既仁慈又美麗，可是也會突然就變得極其殘酷。這些飛翔的小鳥，伴隨著細弱哀婉的鳴叫聲，從空中落下，在海水裡覓食，對大海來說，他們生得過於柔弱了。

他一直把大海看作是 la mar，這是個西班牙語的詞，大家喜歡大海時，就這麼稱呼她。喜歡大海的人，有時也會說她的壞話，不過在他們的談論中，大海總彷彿是一位女性。年輕的漁夫當中，有些人用這個詞的陽性形式，把大海叫作 el mar，那些人用浮筒當魚線的浮標，靠賣鯊魚肝賺了大錢後，就買起了摩托艇。他們談起大海，如同談起一個比賽對手、一處地方，甚至是一個敵人。但是老人一直把大海看作是女性，無論她給予極大的恩惠，或是拒絕給予，或是變得野蠻而邪惡，都是因為她身不由己。他想，月亮影響著她，如同月亮影響著女人。

他平穩地划著小船，保持著均勻的速度，所以也不特別費力。除了偶爾幾個小漩流，海面十分平靜。他讓海流幫著出了三分之一的力氣。天亮的時候，他發現小船已經離岸很遠，超出了自己的預期。

他想，我在大井這一帶忙了整整一個禮拜，卻一無所獲。今天我可要弄清楚那些鰹魚和長鰭鮪魚到底在哪裡，說不定就有條大魚跟他們在一塊兒呢。

沒等到天色大亮，他就放出魚餌，然後順著海流漂浮而去。第一個魚餌放在四十英尋深的地方。第二個放在七十五英尋深的地方。第三個和第四個分別

大海既仁慈又美麗，可是也會突然就變得極其殘酷。

在藍色海水中沉到一百英尋和一百二十五英尋的深處。每個魚餌頭朝下，裡面穿著魚鉤，都已經綁好，還縫得牢牢的，魚鉤突出的部分，鉤彎和鉤尖處，都包了新鮮的沙丁魚。每條沙丁魚都被魚鉤貫穿雙眼，這樣魚的身子在鋼製魚鉤那些突出的部分，就形成了半環形。對一條大魚來說，整個魚鉤無處不是香氣和誘人的美味。

男孩給了他兩條新鮮的小鮪魚，也叫長鰭鮪魚，這兩條魚如鉛錘一樣掛在兩根最深的魚線上，而在另外兩根魚線上，他分別掛上一條大青鰺和一條巴托洛若鰺，儘管這是用過的舊餌，但依然完好，再加上新鮮的沙丁魚，增添了氣味，更有吸引力了。每根魚線都有大號鉛筆那麼粗，繫在一根新取的青木條上，只要魚餌一被拉動或觸碰，都會讓木條朝下彎。每根魚線有兩捲四十英尋的線捲，隨時可以接上其他的備用線捲，如此一來，在必要的情況下，一條魚可以拖出超過三百英尋的魚線。

現在，老人一邊觀察船邊三根木條的動靜，一邊輕輕划動船槳，讓魚線盡量上下垂直，保持在合適的深度。天色已經大亮，太陽眼看就要升起來了。

太陽在海面上微微升起時，老人能看見其他船隻了，那些船低低地浮現在海面上，在較為近岸處，橫跨海流，四散開來。然後太陽更加明亮，耀眼的陽光照射到海面上，隨著太陽完全升起，光滑的海面將陽光反射到他的眼睛裡，尖銳地刺痛眼睛，所以他划船時，避免去直視那些反光。他向海水中俯視，觀察那幾根魚線，它們直直垂入海水深處的黑暗裡。他比任何人都更加用心地讓魚線保持垂直，以便在黑暗的水流中、在每一個他所希望的深度，都有魚餌在等著那裡游動的魚。有些漁夫讓魚線隨海流漂浮，有時魚餌只在六十英尋深的地方，而漁夫會誤以為有一百英尋。

然而，他想，我要讓這些魚線都保持精確。我只是不再那麼幸運了。可是誰知道呢？也許就是今天。每一天都是新的一天。有好運氣當然好。但我寧願做到準確無誤。這樣，當好運來臨時，你已經準備好了。

太陽升起兩個小時了，升到更高的地方，當他向東邊眺望時，陽光已不再那麼刺眼。在他的視野裡，現在只有三條船，看上去就像在低矮處，離他很遠，離海岸更近。

我這一生中，早晨的太陽老是刺痛我的眼睛。他心想，即便如此，我的眼睛還是很好。傍晚時分，我可以直視太陽而不會眼前發黑。傍晚的陽光更有威力，早上的陽光卻令人痛苦。

　　就在這時，他看見一隻軍艦鳥，展開長長的黑色翅膀，在他前方的天空中盤旋。突然間，他雙翅後掠，傾斜著俯衝下去，然後又繼續在空中盤旋。

　　「他逮住什麼啦，」老人大聲說，「他可不僅是看看而已。」

　　他緩慢而穩定地朝著鳥兒盤旋的地方划去。他一點也不匆忙。他讓那些魚線依然保持垂直。不過他稍稍加快了一點速度，想利用那隻鳥兒的引導。雖然稍稍加快了一點，他依然要照著正確的方式行動。

　　那隻鳥兒飛到更高的地方繼續盤旋，他展開的雙翅一動也不動。然後只見他突然俯衝到海裡。老人看見飛魚從海水中疾速躍起，近乎絕望地在海面上掠過。

　　「鯕鰍，」老人大聲說，「大鯕鰍魚！」

　　他擱下雙槳，從船頭下面拿出一套小魚線。這根魚線連著一段金屬前導線和一個中號魚鉤，他在魚鉤上掛上一條沙丁魚做魚餌。他從船的一側放出魚線，將另一端牢牢地固定在船尾一顆帶環的螺栓上。接著，他給另一套捲著的魚線也掛上了魚餌，將它放在船頭的陰影裡。他重新開始划船，並且注視著那

有好運氣當然好。但我寧願做到準確無誤。這樣，當好運來臨時，你已經準備好了。

隻有長長翅膀的黑色鳥兒，此刻，他低飛在水面上，正在覓食。

他正看著的時候，那鳥兒再次傾斜著翅膀，俯衝下來，然後猛烈而無意義地拍打翅膀，追逐飛魚。老人看見水面有些微微隆起，那是大鯕鰍在水中上浮，追逐著逃跑的飛魚。鯕鰍正在飛魚躍起的下方，破水而行，只等飛魚落回水中，他們就會全速追趕。老人心想，這是多大一群鯕鰍啊，他們散布在非常寬廣的一片海水裡，飛魚幾乎沒什麼逃脫的機會。鳥兒沒有機會抓到飛魚。對鳥兒來說，那些飛魚太大，也太快。

他看著飛魚一次又一次飛快地闖出海面，他看著那隻鳥兒徒勞無功的動作，他心想，那一大群鯕鰍已經離我而去了。他們游得那麼快、那麼遠。或許我能抓到一條離群落單的鯕鰍，又或許，我的大魚就在他們附近。我的大魚一定就在某個地方。

此時，雲層如山巒一般在遙遠的陸地上升起，海岸變成了一道長長的綠線，後面是灰藍色的丘陵。此時海水是深藍色的，藍得幾乎發紫。當他俯視海水，看見浮游生物像紅色粉末在幽暗海水中紛紛揚揚，看見照進海水的陽光，此時奇幻如夢。他觀察他的魚線，看見魚線筆直地垂入水下，直至視線之外。

他很高興能看見這麼多浮游生物，因為他知道，這意味著這裡有魚。此時太陽升得更高了，陽光照進海水中產生的奇幻光線，還有陸地上雲層的形狀，都預告著好天氣。可是那隻鳥兒現在幾乎看不到了，水面上也看不到任何東西，只有幾條被曬得發白的黃色海藻和一隻緊挨著船邊漂浮的僧帽水母，牠的膠狀氣囊是紫色的，裝模作樣，閃閃發光。牠來回翻滾著，像個大氣泡似的，愉快地在水中漂浮，那些致命的紫色觸鬚在牠身後蔓延，足有一碼長。

「Agua mala（毒水母），」老人罵道，「你這婊子！」

他輕輕晃動身體，搖著船槳，順著船槳朝水中望去，看見一些小魚，顏色和水裡蔓延的觸鬚差不多，游動在那些觸鬚之間和氣囊漂浮時投下的小小陰影裡。這些小魚對水母的毒素有免疫力。人可沒有。當那些觸鬚纏在魚線上，就會留下紫色的黏液。如果老人釣魚時觸碰到這種黏液，他的手臂和手掌就會紅腫潰瘍，就像觸碰了臭藤和毒葛。而且這種水母的毒素發作得更快，一旦觸碰，就痛得像挨了鞭打一般。

這些閃著虹彩的大氣泡非常美麗。但牠們是海洋中最虛偽的傢伙。老人很樂意看到海龜把牠們吃掉。海龜看到牠們時，就迎面向牠們靠過去，還會閉上

43

眼睛，這樣就能讓自己完全處於龜甲的保護下，然後把牠們連同觸鬚一起吃掉。老人喜歡海龜吃掉牠們，也喜歡在暴風雨過後的海灘上踩著牠們走路，聽牠們在長滿老繭的腳掌下，發出劈劈啪啪的爆裂聲。

他喜愛綠蠵龜和玳瑁，他們優雅而敏捷，價錢又好。對又大又笨的紅海龜，他卻有著善意的輕蔑，因為他們總是膽怯地縮在甲殼裡，做愛的方式也怪怪的，吃水母時，還會幸福地合上眼睛。

雖然他曾經在捕龜船上工作多年，他對海龜倒沒什麼神祕主義的想法。他同情所有的海龜，甚至那些身軀像小船一樣長、體重以噸計的大傢伙。多數人都對海龜很殘忍，因為海龜被剖開、被宰殺之後，心臟還能繼續跳動幾個小時。可是老人想我也有這麼一顆心臟，我也有他們那樣的手和腳。為了讓自己長力氣，他吃白色的海龜蛋。他整個五月都吃海龜蛋，好讓自己在九月和十月裡足夠強壯，可以應付真正的大魚。

在許多漁夫存放漁具的棚屋裡，他每天都從大圓桶裡舀一杯鯊魚肝油喝下去。鯊魚肝油就在那兒，漁夫誰想喝就喝。多數漁夫都討厭那個味道。可是這也不會比那麼早就要起床更難受，何況鯊魚肝油能抵禦風寒和流感，還對眼睛有好處。

此刻老人抬頭望去，看見那隻鳥又在空中盤旋。

「他已經找到魚啦！」他大聲道。這時並沒有飛魚衝破水面，也沒有四散開去的小魚。然而就在老人觀察的時候，一條鮪魚躍上空中，一轉身，頭朝下扎入水中。那條鮪魚在陽光下銀光閃耀，他扎入水中後，又有一些鮪魚，一條接一條從水裡跳出來，他們到處都是，跳動著，攪動著海水，還追著魚餌跳得老遠。他們圍繞著魚餌，追趕著魚餌。

老人心想，要不是他們游得太快，我就趕上他們了。他注視著這群鮪魚攪得海水變成白色，這時那隻鳥也俯衝下來，啄食那些在驚慌中被迫浮向水面的小魚。

「這鳥可真幫了大忙。」老人說。就在這時，船尾那根魚線在他腳下突然繃緊了。之前他在那根魚線上結了一個圈，套在腳上。他放下船槳，握緊魚線，當他著手收回魚線時，感覺到小鮪魚顫抖的拉力。他用力往回收線，那顫抖越發劇烈。在他將魚越過船舷甩進船艙前，他看見了水中那條魚藍色的背和金色的兩側。現在那條魚躺在船尾，在陽光裡，他顯得短小精悍，形如子彈，瞪

45

著一雙無知的大眼睛，正用他光滑靈活的尾巴，帶著顫抖，快速拍打著船板，像是要把自己的生命拍打出來似的。出於仁慈，老人照他頭上打了一下，然後把他踢到船尾的陰涼處，而他的身體依然顫抖著。

「長鰭鮪魚，」他大聲說，「可以用他做個漂亮的魚餌。看起來有十磅重。」

他記不起自己究竟什麼時候開始，在獨處的時候，會大聲對自己說話。從前當他孤身一人時，他總是唱歌，有時還會在夜裡唱歌，那是他在小漁船或者捕龜船上值班的時候。大概是在那男孩離開他之後，他開始一個人大聲自言自語的吧。但他已經不記得了。他和男孩一起釣魚時，通常只在必要時才說話。他們在夜裡說話，或是在壞天氣裡受困於暴風雨的時候。在海上，少言寡語被視為美德。老人對此一向認同，並且尊重。可是現在他已經許多次大聲說出心裡所想的，反正他也不會打擾到任何人。

「如果別人聽到我這樣大聲自言自語，一定當我瘋了，」他大聲說，「既然我沒有真的發瘋，我才不在乎他們怎麼想。有錢人的船上有無線電和他們說話，還能帶來棒球賽的消息呢。」

現在可不是想棒球的時候，他想。現在只能去想唯一一件事。那是我天生要做的事。也許那魚群的附近就有一條大魚。在那群正在捕食的鮪魚中，我只是抓到一條掉隊離群的。可是現在他們游出遠去捕食了，游得很快。今天海面上出現的所有東西都游得很快，都往東北方向游去。難道一天中的某個時刻就會如此？或者，這是某種我不懂的天氣徵兆？

這時候他已經看不到海岸的綠色了，只能看見藍色山丘的頂部，顯出白色，彷彿覆蓋了積雪，而那上方的雲層，看起來像是高聳的雪山。海水的顏色很幽暗，陽光在其中變化多端。太陽升高了，數不清的浮游生物的微粒，都消隱不見了，老人只看到藍色海水裡延伸到深處的絢麗的巨大光帶，還有他的幾根魚線，筆直垂入水中，垂到很深很深的地方。

鮪魚沉回深處去了。漁夫把所有這種類型的魚都叫作鮪魚，只有拿去售賣或者交換魚餌時，才用正式名稱把他們區分開來。這會兒太陽變得炙熱了，老人划船時，能感覺到脖頸後面陽光的曝曬，還有背後緩緩滴落的汗水。

我本可以讓小船就這樣順水漂著，他想，我可以把魚線繫在腳趾上，一有動靜就能把我弄醒。但今天是第八十五天了，今天一整天，我都應該好好釣魚。

47

就在這時，當他注視著魚線，他看見伸向水面的青木條當中，有一根正急劇地下沉。

「來了，」他說，「來了！」他放下手中的船槳，沒讓小船有一絲顛簸，然後伸手抓起魚線，將魚線輕輕地握在右手的拇指和食指之間。這時魚線又動了一下。他沒有感覺到張力，也沒有感覺到重量。他輕輕握著魚線。這時魚線又動了一下。這是試探性的一拉，既不強硬，也不沉重。但他確知這是怎麼一回事了。在一百英尋的海水深處，一條馬林魚正在吃魚鉤上的沙丁魚，那些沙丁魚包裹著鉤尖和鉤柄，正是手工打製的魚鉤穿過一條小鮪魚頭部後，突出在外面的部分。

老人仔細而輕柔地握著魚線，用左手將魚線從木條上解下來。這樣魚線就可以在他的手指間快速滑動，而不會讓魚感覺到任何張力。

離岸如此遠，又在這樣的月分，他一定非常大，他想。吃吧，魚兒。請你吃了他們吧。這些沙丁魚多麼新鮮，而你孤零零待在六百英尺深的又暗又冷的海水裡。你在黑暗中再再轉一圈，回來吧，把他們吃了吧。

他感覺到魚線被很輕、很小心地拉動了一下，接著是更有力的一次，或許是其中一條沙丁魚的頭更難從魚鉤上扯落吧。然後一切都安靜了。

「快來呀，」老人大聲說，「轉身回來吧，聞一聞這些沙丁魚，多麼鮮美。趁著新鮮吃了吧。吃完了還有鮪魚，吃起來又結實又爽口，而且也很鮮美呢。別害羞，魚兒。吃了吧。」

他將魚線握在大拇指和食指之間，等待著，在注視這根魚線的同時，也觀察著其他魚線，因為這條魚說不定會上下游動。這時魚線又像剛才那樣，被很小心地拉了一下。

「他會吃的，」老人大聲說，「上帝保佑他吃吧。」

但是他依然沒有吃，他游走了。老人感覺不到任何動靜了。

「他不可能游走的，」他說，「天曉得，他不可能游走的。他只是轉一圈罷了。也許他以前曾經上過鉤，到現在還心有餘悸吧。」

這時候他感覺到魚線再次被輕柔地觸碰。他十分高興。

「他剛才只是轉了一圈，」他說，「他會吃的。」

他十分高興地感受著魚線輕柔的拉動，然後他感覺到這拉動變得有力而沉重，沉重得令人難以置信。這是那條魚本身的重量，所以他讓魚線往下滑動，往下，往下，兩捲備用魚線中的一捲都放下去了。當魚線往下滑動，當它從老

49

人手指間輕輕滑過時，儘管老人在大拇指與食指間施加的壓力微乎其微，還是感覺到極大的重量。

「好一條大魚啊，」他說，「他把魚餌斜叼在嘴裡，他正要帶著魚餌離開呢。」

接著他就會轉過身來吞吃魚餌了，他想。他沒有把這個想法說出來，因為他知道，如果你說破了一件好事，那好事就不會發生了。他知道這是多麼巨大的一條魚，他想像那條魚嘴巴裡斜叼著鮪魚，在黑暗中企圖離開。就在那一瞬間，他感覺他停止游動，然而那重量依然還在。接著他感到重量不斷增加，就放出更多魚線。他加大了拇指與食指之間的力道，片刻間，魚線越來越重，直向深處墜去。

「他上鉤了，」他說，「現在我要讓他把魚餌好好吃下去。」

他讓魚線在他的手指間滑動。與此同時，他向下伸出左手，將這根魚線的兩捲備用魚線空出來的一頭，牢牢繫在為另一根魚線準備的兩捲備用魚線的繩圈裡。現在他準備好了。除了手上正在用的那捲魚線，他還有三捲四十英尋的魚線可供備用呢。

「再多吃一點，」他說，「好好吃。」

把魚餌吃下去，魚鉤的鉤尖就會刺進你的心臟、就會殺死你，他想。然後乖乖浮上水面，讓我將魚叉扎進你的身體。就是這樣。你準備好了嗎？這頓美味，你吃得夠久了嗎？

「時候到了！」他大聲喊著，雙手用力，將魚線往回收了一碼，然後再收，再收，他雙臂交替擺動著，一次又一次，往回拉動魚線，不僅使出了雙臂的力氣，還加上回轉身體的力量。

然而，什麼也沒發生。那條魚只是慢慢地游開去，老人竟不能把他向上拉動一英寸。他的魚線很結實，是用來釣大魚的。他把魚線勒在背上，魚線緊繃，甚至都迸出了水珠。隨後魚線在水裡慢慢發出嘶嘶的響聲。他依然沒有鬆手，以小船的橫座板為支撐，身體盡力後仰，用後背抵抗著魚線的張力。小船漸漸離開原地，向西北方向移動。

大魚很穩定地游著，他們在平靜的水面上緩緩行進。其他幾個魚餌還在水裡，但他已經無暇顧及了。

「真希望男孩在這兒，」老人大聲道，「我竟被一條魚拖著走，簡直成了

51

拴繩子的纜柱了！我可以把魚線固定住，但那樣就會被魚掙斷。我要盡可能把魚線抓在手裡，必要的時候放出一些才行。感謝上帝，他在朝前游，而不是往下去。」

如果那魚打算往下去，我還真不知道該怎麼辦。如果他潛入海底，死在那裡，我也不知道該怎麼辦。不過我總該做點什麼。我能做的事情還有很多。

他把魚線勒在後背上，注視著魚線在海水中的傾斜，而小船正平穩地向西北方向移動。

這會讓那條魚送命的。老人想，他不可能一直拖著小船跑。然而過了四個小時之後，那條魚照樣拖著小船，慢條斯理地，游向大海更遠處。老人也依然將魚線勒在後背上，頑強支撐著。

「我中午就釣上這條魚了，」他說，「到現在我還沒見過他呢。」

沒釣上大魚之前，他一直把頭上的草帽使勁往前拉，現在那草帽正割痛他的前額。而且他覺得口渴了，於是他雙膝跪下，小心地不去扯動魚線，盡可能挪向船頭，伸出一隻手，摳向裝水的瓶子。他打開瓶蓋，喝了點水。然後他坐在捲著船帆的桅杆上，靠著船頭休息，努力讓自己什麼都不想，只是忍耐。

52

他回頭望去，早已看不見陸地。這倒沒什麼差別，他想。依靠哈瓦那的燈火，我總能順利回港。離太陽下山還有兩個小時，也許在那之前，這條大魚就會浮出水面。如果他還不上來，也許會隨著明天的太陽一起出來。我沒有抽筋，而且感覺自己很強壯。上來，也許會隨著月亮一起出來；如果他不隨著月亮被魚鉤鉤著嘴巴的可是他呀。不過能有力氣拖著小船游這麼長時間，那該是怎樣的一條魚啊！他一定用嘴巴死死咬住了魚鉤上的鋼絲。我多麼希望看見他，哪怕看見一次，我就能知道，我有怎樣一個對手了。

依靠對天上星辰的觀察，老人可以看出，那條魚一整夜都沒有改變路線和方向。太陽下山後，海上很冷。老人身上的汗水都乾了，這讓他的後背和手臂還有兩條老腿，都覺得格外寒冷。白天的時候，老人把蓋在魚餌盒子上的麻袋拿下來，攤在陽光下曬乾。太陽下山後，他把麻袋繫在脖子上、披在背後。這會兒，他小心翼翼地將麻袋塞到勒在肩膀上的魚線下面。有麻袋墊著魚線，而且他還找到一種方式，將身體前傾靠在船頭，這樣一來，他幾乎覺得自己很舒服。這種姿勢充其量只是不再那麼難以忍受罷了，但是他認為，能這樣就算很舒服了。

我拿他沒有辦法，他也拿我沒有辦法，他想。這條魚要是一直這麼下去，誰都沒辦法。

有一次他站起身來，在船舷邊撒尿，抬頭瞭望星星，確認自己現在的航向。魚線像一道磷光，從他肩膀上筆直延伸到海水裡。他們現在移動得更加緩慢了，哈瓦那的燈火已經越來越微弱，於是他知道，一定是海流正把他們帶往偏東的方向。他想，如果我看不見哈瓦那的燈火，一定是因為我們正在往東去。假如沿著大魚原來的路線，我還會有很長時間能看到哈瓦那的燈火。我很想知道棒球大聯盟今天的比賽結果。釣魚時能有臺無線電該是多麼美妙。然後他又轉念道，你要永遠想著一件事，那就是你正在做的事，它不容有錯。

隨即他大聲說：「我真希望那個男孩在這裡，幫幫我，看看我正在做的這一切！」

任何人到了老年，都不應該孤單，他想。然而這件事無法避免。我一定要記住，趁鮪魚還沒爛掉，就把他吃下去，好保持體力。要記住，不管你多麼不想吃，明天早上也要把他吃下去。他對自己說，千萬要記住。

在夜間，有兩隻鼠海豚來到小船附近，他能聽見他們在海裡打滾和噴水的聲音。他能分辨出兩隻鼠海豚不同的噴水聲，公海豚發出很大聲響，母海豚則輕如歎息。

「他們真好，」他說，「他們嬉戲打鬧，他們彼此相愛。他們像飛魚一樣，是我們的兄弟。」

接著他開始同情他到的這條大魚。他既美妙又奇怪，誰知道他有多大年紀呢？我還從來沒有過如此強壯的魚，也沒見過行為如此奇怪的魚。也許他太聰明了，所以不願意跳出海面。他只要跳出海面，或者往前猛衝，就會讓我無法招架。也許他以前很多次被魚鉤困住過，他知道該用怎樣的方式來戰鬥。他無法知道的是，他所對付的只是單獨一人，而且是個老人。但他真是一條了不起的大魚，如果肉質夠新鮮，他在市場上能賣出怎樣的好價錢啊。他吞吃魚餌的方式像公魚，他拉動魚線的方式像公魚，他在戰鬥中沒有一絲慌亂。我真想知道，他究竟是有什麼想好的計畫，還是和我一樣，僅僅出於絕望，才鋌而走險？

他還記得有一回他釣到一對馬林魚的其中一條。在馬林魚中，公魚總是讓母魚先進食，而上鉤的那一條正是母魚，她驚慌失措，瘋狂而絕望的掙扎很快就讓她筋疲力竭了。那條公魚始終待在她的身邊，在魚線邊穿來穿去，和她一起在海面上轉圈。公魚離魚線很近，老人很擔心他的尾巴會割斷魚線，他尾巴的形狀和大小都像一把長柄大鐮刀，而且鋒利異常。老人用拖鉤把母魚拖上來，用棍子打她，又握住她形如細劍、邊緣像砂紙般割手的長嘴，敲擊她的頭部，直到她的顏色變得如同鏡子背面的顏色一樣，才在男孩的幫助下，把她拖進船艙。直到那時，公魚還待在船邊沒有離開。後來，當老人整理魚線和魚叉時，公魚從船邊高高跳上空中，想看看母魚在哪兒，然後沉入了深處。他淡紫色的翅膀，也就是他的胸鰭，充分地展開著，所有寬寬的淡紫色條紋都顯露出來。他真漂亮，老人記得，他不忍離去。

老人想，這是我在魚身上見過最悲傷的事情了。男孩也很悲傷，因此我們請求母魚原諒，當即就把她宰殺了。

「我真希望男孩能在這兒。」他大聲說著，把身體倚靠在船頭的圓弧形木板上，透過勒在肩膀上的魚線，他感受到大魚的力量，這股力量讓他們一起向著大魚選擇的方向平穩地移動著。

一旦中了我的圈套，他就不得不做出選擇了，老人心想。

他的選擇就是堅持留在黑暗的深水裡，遠離一切圈套、陷阱和詭計。我的選擇是超越所有人，到他藏身的地方找到他。超越世界上所有的人。現在我們結合在一起，而且從中午開始就這樣了。並且，我們各自都孤立無援。

也許我本不該當漁夫，他想。但我就是為此而生的。我要確確實實地記住，天亮之後就把鮪魚吃下去。

天亮之前的某個時刻，有什麼東西咬住了他身後一根魚線上的魚餌。他聽到木條折斷的聲音，那根魚線越過船舷飛快地向海裡滑去。在黑暗中，他從刀鞘中拔出刀子，用左肩承擔起大魚所有的拉力，身體往後傾斜，就著船舷的木板，用刀子將那根魚線割斷。然後又割斷離他最近的另一根魚線，在黑暗中摸索著，將兩捲備用魚線的斷頭繫在一起。他只用一隻手就熟練地完成了這一切。他用一隻腳踩在備用線捲上，穩住它們，拉緊繫好的繩結。現在他有六捲備用魚線了。每根割斷的魚線都有兩捲備用魚線，釣著大魚的這一根也有兩捲，它們全都接在一起了。

等天亮以後，他想，我要把魚餌放在四十英尋深處的魚線也割斷，把那兩捲備用魚線也接上。這樣一來，我會損失兩百英尋上好的加泰隆尼亞魚線，還有魚鉤和魚鉤上的金屬前導線。這些都可以重新置備。如果我為了釣別的魚而讓釣上大魚的這根魚線被弄斷、讓大魚逃脫了，誰來補償這樣的損失呢？我不知道剛才咬餌的是什麼，有可能是一條馬林魚、一條劍魚，或者是一條鯊魚。我根本沒有時間去感覺他，因為我必須盡快擺脫他。

他大聲說：「要是那個男孩在這裡就好了！」

可是那個男孩並不在你身邊，他想。你只有你自己，你最好現在就去收拾最後剩下的那根魚線，不管天亮還是天黑，你要把它割斷，把那兩捲備用魚線也接上。

於是他就這樣做了。在黑暗中做這些真是很困難，而且那魚突然間向前猛竄了一下，將他臉朝下拉倒在船上，他的眼睛下方破了一道口子。鮮血沿著臉頰流下來，但還沒有流到下巴那兒，就凝結起來，乾掉了。他設法挪回船頭，靠在木板上休息。他調整好麻袋，很小心地將魚線在肩上挪了一下位置。他一邊仔細地感受著大魚的拉力，一邊將手伸進水裡，感受小船前進的狀態。

不知道那魚剛才為什麼突然猛竄那麼一下，他想。一定是鋼絲在他高高隆起的脊背上滑過的緣故。他背上的疼痛一定比不上我背上的疼痛吧。但是不管他有多大，他也不可能永遠拖著小船跑。現在我已經清理掉所有會惹麻煩的東西了，而且我還有足夠的備用魚線；一切令人滿意。

「魚啊，」他溫柔地，卻是大聲地說，「我死也要和你待在一起。」

我猜他也不會離開我的，老人這樣想著，等待著天亮。眼下是天亮前最冷的時候，他將身體緊貼著船板取暖。他想，魚能堅持多久，我就能堅持多久。

在第一縷陽光中，魚線延伸出去，沉入水中。小船平穩地移動著，當太陽露出最初的邊緣，陽光正好照在老人右邊的肩膀上。

「他在朝北去啊。」老人說。海流會把我們遠遠地帶往東邊，他想。我真希望他順著海流改變方向。那樣就說明他越來越疲乏了。

當太陽高高升起，老人卻發現大魚一點也不疲乏。眼下只有一個有利的徵兆。魚線的傾斜角度，表明大魚在比原來更淺一些的地方游動。這不一定表示他會跳到水面上來，卻有這種可能。

「上帝啊，讓他跳吧，」老人說，「我有足夠長的魚線來對付他。」

也許我把魚線拉得再緊一點，就會弄痛他，就會讓他跳出來，他想。既然現在已經是白天了，就讓他跳吧，這樣他脊骨兩側的魚鰾裡就會充滿空氣，他

59

就不可能沉到海底去死在那兒了。

他試著將魚線拉得更緊一些，可是自從他釣上這條魚以來，魚線就一直繃得很緊，幾乎要繃斷，所以當他後仰著身體拉動魚線時，感到魚線無比堅硬，就知道自己不可能把他拉得更緊了。我絕不可以突然猛拉一氣，他想。每一次突然的猛拉，都會讓魚鉤造成的傷口裂得更寬，等他真的跳出水面時，就有可能把魚鉤甩掉的。好在陽光讓我感覺舒服多了，而且至少此刻我無須一直盯著他了。

魚線上粘了一些黃色的海藻，老人對此倒是高興的，因為他知道，這對魚來說是額外的負擔。正是這種墨西哥灣的黃色海藻，在夜間發出很強的磷光。

「魚啊，」他說，「我很愛你，也很尊重你。可是今天結束之前，我一定要殺死你。」

但願如此，他想。

一隻小鳥從北方向小船飛來。那是一隻小小的鳴禽，他低低地飛行在水面上。老人看得出那鳥兒非常疲勞。

鳥兒飛到船尾，在那兒歇息片刻，然後繞著老人頭頂飛了一圈，落在那根魚線上，似乎覺得那裡更舒服。

「你有多大了？」老人問鳥兒，「這是你第一次出門遠行嗎？」

他說話的時候，鳥兒一直看著他。他太累了，來不及仔細查看這根魚線，就用纖細的爪子緊緊抓住，在上面晃來晃去。

「魚線很穩的，」老人告訴他，「穩極了。昨天夜裡一點風都沒有，你不該累成這樣啊。鳥兒也不如從前了嗎？」

他想，那些飛到海上來的老鷹，會撞見這些小鳥的。他沒跟小鳥說這些，反正他也聽不懂，何況他很快就要領教老鷹的厲害了。

「好好歇會兒吧，小鳥，」他說，「然後你就得繼續往前，去試試自己的運氣了，就像每一個人、每一隻鳥或者每一條魚那樣。」

他的背僵直了一整夜，這會兒正痛得厲害，和鳥兒說說話，讓他精神起來。

「如果你願意，就住在我家吧，鳥兒，」他說，「可惜我不能趁著現在吹來的微風升起帆來迎接你。因為我正在接待一個朋友。」

就在這時候，大魚突然一個頓挫，把老人拖倒在船頭上。要不是老人撐住身子，及時放出一些魚線，恐怕就被拖到海裡去了。

魚線被突然拉動時，鳥兒就飛走了，老人甚至來不及看到他離去。他用右手小心地觸摸一下魚線，卻發現自己的手在流血。

「一定是什麼東西把他弄痛了。」他大聲說，同時他試著將魚線往回拉，看看是否能讓魚轉變方向。當他感覺到魚線快要斷裂的極限時，就用手穩住魚線，仰坐著，頂住魚線的張力。

「魚啊，你現在感覺到痛了吧，」他說，「上帝知道，我也一樣啊！」

他環顧四周，尋找那隻小鳥，他已經喜歡上有他做伴了。可是鳥兒已經飛走了。

你在這兒沒待多久啊，老人想。在你飛到岸上之前，還要經歷更多艱難呢。我怎麼能讓那魚一個猛拉就弄傷自己呢？我一定是越來越蠢了。要不，就是因為我看著那小鳥，把心思放到了他的身上。現在我必須把注意力集中到工作上來，我還必須把鮪魚吃下去，這樣才不會缺少力氣。

「要是男孩在這兒就好了，要是我帶些鹽來就好了。」他大聲說。

他將魚線的重量挪到左邊肩膀上，然後小心地跪下來，在海水中洗手。他讓手浸泡在海水裡，超過一分鐘，著小船的行進，海水平穩地沖刷著他的手。他讓手浸泡在海水裡，超過一分鐘，看著血跡在海水裡漸漸消失。

「他已經游得慢多了。」他說。

老人很想讓他的手在海水裡多泡一會兒，可是他擔心那魚再突然來一次猛拉，就站起身來，穩住自己，對著太陽舉起那隻受傷的手。只不過是被繃緊的魚線割破了皮肉，然而卻傷在了做事時要用到的地方。他知道自己需要這雙手，直到弄完這一切；他不喜歡一切還沒開始前，自己的手就被弄傷了。

「這會兒呢，」等手晾乾了，他說，「我得吃這條小鮪魚了。我可以用拖鉤把他拖過來，然後在這兒舒舒服服地吃。」

他跪下來，用拖鉤在船尾找到那條鮪魚，將牠朝自己這邊拉過來，小心翼翼地不讓牠碰到那些備用魚線。他再次用左肩拉住魚線，以左手和左臂為支撐，把鮪魚從拖鉤的鉤齒上取下，又將拖鉤放回了原處。他用一邊的膝蓋壓在魚的身上，然後從頭到尾，沿著魚的脊背，縱向割下一條條深紅的魚肉。魚肉被割成了楔形，他沿著脊骨一直割到了魚肚子的邊緣。割下六條魚肉之後，他將這些魚肉在船頭木板上攤開，在褲子上擦了擦刀子，然後拎起魚尾巴，把魚骨扔到海裡。

「我可不認為自己能吃下完整的一條。」他一邊說著，一邊用刀子將一條魚肉切成兩半。他可以感覺到魚線穩定而沉重的拉力，還感覺到他的左手抽起筋來。他的左手在粗魚線上緊緊地抽成一團。他充滿厭惡地看著那隻手。

「這算哪門子的手啊，」他說，「你要抽筋就隨便抽吧。把自己弄成一副鳥爪子模樣，對你有什麼好！」

快點吧，他心想。他順著傾斜的魚線，向黑暗的深水裡望去。現在就吃吧，這些魚肉會讓你的手恢復力量的。其實也不能怪這隻手，你和大魚已經僵持了好多個小時了。當然，你完全能夠和他永遠僵持下去。快把鮪魚吃了吧。

他撿起一片魚肉，放進嘴裡，慢慢咀嚼著。倒也不那麼難吃。

好好嚼一嚼，他想，把汁都嚼出來。要是能放上點萊姆或者檸檬，或者放點鹽，味道就更好了。

「手啊，你感覺怎樣啊？」他向那隻抽筋的手問道，而它僵硬得如一具死屍，「我會為了你再多吃一點。」

他把剛才切好的另一半魚肉也吃了。他仔細地咀嚼著，然後把魚皮吐了出來。

「覺得怎麼樣了呢，手？或許現在還不知道吧？」

他又拿起一整條魚肉，放進嘴裡嚼起來。

「他真是一條強壯而鮮活的魚啊，」他想，「我很幸運，釣到了他，而不是鯕鰍。鯕鰍的肉太甜了，而這條魚幾乎一點都不泛甜，還保留了十足的韌勁。」

「任何東西，只有實用才有意義，他想。真希望我能有點鹽。我不知道太陽會不會把剩下的魚肉給曬爛，或者曬乾。所以我最好把這些魚肉都吃下去。雖然我現在還不覺得餓。那條大魚現在很平靜、很穩定。我要把剩下的全吃掉，那樣我就不慌了。

「有點耐心吧，手，」他說，「我做這些是為了你啊！」

我真希望也能餵一餵那條大魚，他想。他是我的兄弟。可是我必須殺死他，還要保持精力來做這件事。他緩慢而盡責地把那些楔形的條狀魚肉全都吃了下去。

他伸直了腰，在褲子上擦手。

「現在，」他說，「你可以放下魚線了，手啊，在你停止胡鬧之前，我會用右手單獨對付他。」他用左腳踩住原來由左手握著的粗魚線，身體向後仰，抵抗著魚線在後背上的拉力。

「上帝幫幫我，讓我別再抽筋了吧！」他說，「誰都不知道那魚接下來還要怎樣呢。」

可是他看起來很鎮定，好像照著他自己的計畫在行動，他想。但他的計畫是什麼呢？

我又有什麼計畫呢？他想。我的計畫只好跟著他的計畫隨機應變，因為他的體型實在太大了。如果他跳出水面，我就能殺死他。可是，如果他堅持待在水下，我也只好堅持下去，奉陪到底。

他在褲子上來回摩擦那隻抽筋的手，想要讓手指變得柔軟。然而那隻手還是無法張開。也許在太陽下曬著，它就會張開，他想。也許等我消化了那些強壯的生魚肉，這隻手就能張開了。如果我不得不用這隻手，我就要張開它，不管要付出多大代價。不過眼下，我還不想強行張開它。還是等它自己張開，讓它聽從自己的意願吧。不管怎麼說，昨天夜裡我把它用得太狠了，又要釋放魚線、又要防止幾條魚線相互糾結。

他放眼向海面上望去，發現自己此刻竟如此孤單。但是他能在幽暗深邃的海水裡看見彩虹，看見筆直向前延伸的魚線，還看見平靜海面上奇異的波動。海上漸漸吹起信風，讓雲朵積聚起來。他向前方望去，看見一群海鴨飛過海水上方，他們的身影，刻畫在天空背景中，一時鮮明，一時黯淡，然後又鮮明起來。於是他知道，沒有誰在海上會永遠孤單。

他想起，有些人多麼害怕讓小船去往看不見陸地的地方，他知道在那些天氣會突如其來變得糟糕的月分裡，那些人的擔心是有道理的。但如今正是刮颶風的月分，在這樣的月分，如果沒有颶風，就會是一年當中天氣最好的時候。

如果要刮颶風，而你又正好在海上，就會提前幾天看到各種預兆出現在天空中。待在岸上的人卻看不出來，因為他們不知道該看什麼，他想。陸地一定也會改變這些雲彩的形狀吧。可是現在，我們不會遇上颶風的。

他抬頭向天空中望去，看見積聚起來的白色雲朵彷彿是一大團可愛的冰淇淋，而在更高處，則是稀疏羽毛般的捲雲，映襯著九月的萬里晴空。

「吹起了東北風，」他說，「魚啊，這樣的天氣對我來說是好事，對你來說可算不上什麼好事啊。」

67

他的左手還抽著筋，但是他正慢慢地將它舒展開。

我真討厭抽筋，他想。這就是自己的身體在背叛自己。要是因為食物中毒導致腹瀉或者嘔吐，那是在人前丟臉；然而要是抽筋，他想起抽筋時用的是西班牙語的 calambre，就是自己在羞辱自己，尤其當一個人獨自待著的時候。

如果男孩在這兒，他會替我按摩一下，好讓我從小臂起都放鬆下來，他想。

不過它總會放鬆下來的。

這時，他的右手感覺到魚線上的拉力起了變化，然後他看見魚線在水裡的傾斜角度也在改變。當他倚靠著魚線，將左手快速地在大腿上狠狠拍打的時候，看見傾斜的魚線正緩慢地向上升起。

「他要上來了，」他說，「手啊，快點，請你快點好吧！」

魚線緩慢而平穩地升起，接著船頭前的海水鼓了起來，那條魚浮出了水面。他的上浮過程幾乎無休無止，水流從他身體兩側傾瀉而下。他在陽光下閃發光，他的腦袋和背部是深紫色，而身體兩側的條紋，呈現出薰衣草般淡淡的紫色，在陽光下顯得很寬闊。他的尖嘴有棒球棍那麼長，逐漸變細，像一把長劍。他的整個身體完整地浮出水面之後，又流暢地重返水中，像一艘潛艇。

老人看到他那大鐮刀般的尾巴沒入水下，魚線也開始飛快地滑動。

「他比這小船還要長上兩英尺呢。」老人說。魚線滑得很快卻很平穩，說明這魚一點也不慌張。老人試著用雙手拉住魚線，又要確保魚線不被拉斷。他明白，要平穩地施加壓力，讓這魚慢下來。否則他就會把所有魚線都拉出去，還會把魚線弄斷。

這是一條大魚，我一定要制伏他，他想。我一定不能讓他瞭解自身有多強大，也不能讓他知道，如果他全力逃跑，事情會怎樣。如果換了我是他，現在我就會孤注一擲，拚命向前，直到魚線被弄斷。可是，感謝上帝，他並沒有我們這些要殺他的人聰明；儘管他們比人更高貴，更有才能。

老人也見過不少大魚。他見過不少重量超過一千磅的大魚，還抓到過兩條那麼大的，不過都不是獨自一人。現在他是獨自一人，看不見陸地，和一條大魚緊緊糾纏著，這魚是他見過最大的魚，甚至比他聽說過的還要大。而他的左手，緊縮著，像老鷹緊縮的爪子一般。

這隻手的抽筋會好的，他想。左手的抽筋一定會好，那樣就能幫助我的右手。有三樣東西是兄弟：那條魚，和我的兩隻手。這時候抽筋也太說不過去了。

這時，那魚又重新慢了下來，恢復了原來的速度。

我真弄不懂他為什麼要跳出水面，老人想。他跳上來好像就為了給我看看他有多麼大。總之我現在是知道了，他想。真希望我也能讓他瞭解我是怎樣的人，不過那樣他會看到我抽筋的手。還是讓他以為我是更強壯的人吧。我會比現在更強壯的。但願我是那條魚，他想，那條魚竭盡全力要對付的，只不過是我一個人的決心和智慧。

他讓自己舒服地靠在木板上，忍受著不時襲來的疼痛。那魚平穩地游著，小船在幽暗深邃的海面上緩緩前進。東邊吹來的風，讓海面上起了小小的波浪。到了中午，老人的左手不再抽筋了。

「魚啊，這對你來說可是壞消息。」他說著，將魚線在蓋著肩部的麻袋上換了換位置。

他覺得舒服，但又忍受著疼痛，儘管他根本就不承認這疼痛的存在。

「我沒那麼虔誠，」他說，「但是如果能抓住這條魚，我就念十遍天主經和十遍聖母經，如果抓住他，我還會去朝拜科布萊聖母，我發誓。」

他開始機械式地念起禱告來。有時因為太過疲倦，他竟然記不起禱告詞。

於是他就故意念得特別快，讓句子自動地順口溜出來。萬福瑪利亞要比我們在天之父好念些，他想。

「萬福瑪利亞，滿被聖寵者；主於爾偕焉；女中爾為讚美，爾胎子耶穌，並為讚美。天主聖母瑪利亞，為我罪人，今祈天主，及我等死候。阿們。」

然後他又加上兩句，「萬福童貞聖母，求你讓這條大魚死去吧，雖然他是那樣美好。」

當他念完祈禱，感覺好多了，然而疼痛依舊，也許還更屬害了一些。他靠在船頭的木板上，開始機械式地活動著左手的手指。

儘管微風正輕柔地吹過，但此時的陽光已經變得灼熱。

「我最好還是把船尾那根小魚線重新裝上魚餌吧，」他說，「如果那魚打算再這樣耗上一夜的話，我就需要再吃點東西，瓶裡的水也不多了。除了鰦鰍，我在這兒也釣不到別的了。可是如果趁著新鮮吃，鰦鰍的味道也不算差。我希望今天夜裡能有條飛魚跳到船上來。可惜我沒有燈光來吸引他們。飛魚生吃起來很美味，而且還無需我切成小塊。現在我得保存好所有的體力。上帝啊，我可不知道那魚竟有如此巨大。」

「那我也得殺了他，」他說，「不管他有多麼巨大、多麼了不起。」

雖然這很不公平，他想。但我要讓他知道，一個人能做到什麼，能忍受什麼。

「我對男孩說過，我是個不同尋常的老頭子，」他說，「現在是我證明這一點的時候。」

他已經證明過上千次了，但那不算什麼。如今他要再一次證明。每一次都是重新來過，當他這麼做的時候，他從不回想過去。

但願那魚會睡覺，這樣我也可以睡覺，夢見那些獅子。為什麼夢裡留下的最重要的東西是那些獅子呢？別想了，老傢伙，他對自己說。靠著船頭，靜靜地休息吧，什麼也別想。那魚正忙著呢。你就盡量歇著吧。

時間已到了下午，小船依舊緩慢而平穩地前進。不過，從東邊吹來的微風給小船增添了阻力，老人在不大的風浪中漂浮，斜勒在後背上的魚線，也不再讓他那麼疼痛、那麼難以忍受了。

下午某一個時候，魚線再次開始上升。但是，那魚只不過在水面下稍高一些的地方繼續往前游。陽光照著老人左邊的手臂和肩膀，還有他的後背，所以

72

他知道，那魚游動的路線，已轉成了東北方向。

既然那魚他已見過一回，他現在就可以想像他在水裡游動的情景了。我很想知道他在那樣的深處能看見多少東西，老人想。那魚的眼睛極大，而一匹馬的眼睛要小得多，都能在黑暗裡看見東西。從前我的眼睛在黑暗中也能看得很清楚。不是說絕對的黑暗。但也和一隻貓的視力相差無幾。

於是他嘗試將魚線的張力更多交給左手。他聳一聳背上的肌肉，稍稍轉移一下魚線造成的疼痛。

他那抽筋的左手，由於陽光照射，加上他持續活動手指，已經完全恢復了。

「你要是還不覺得累，魚啊，」他大聲說，「那你真是太不同尋常啦！」

這時他感到特別累，而且他知道，夜晚就快要降臨了，所以他努力去想些別的事情。他想起職棒大聯盟，他稱之為 Gran Ligas，他知道紐約洋基隊正在迎戰底特律老虎隊。

現在已經是第二天了，但我還不知道 juegos（比賽）的結果呢，他想。然而我必須有信心，我必須配得上偉大的狄馬喬，即使腳後跟長了骨刺，他也忍著疼痛，把所有事情都做得完美無瑕。什麼是骨刺呢？他問自己。Un espuela de hueso（骨刺）。我們身上沒有。它會不會像鬥雞腳上的鐵刺扎進我們腳跟那樣疼痛呢？我覺得自己無法忍受那樣的疼痛，也無法像鬥雞那樣，被啄掉一隻眼珠甚至兩隻眼珠還繼續戰鬥。與偉大的鳥獸相比，人並沒有多少優越之處。比較起來，我還是更願意做那隻待在海水深處的黑暗中的動物。

「除非是來了鯊魚，」他大聲說，「如果來了鯊魚，願上帝憐憫他，也憐憫我。」

你相信偉大的狄馬喬會像我這樣，和一條大魚相持這麼長的時間嗎？我相信他可以，而且能堅持更長的時間，因為他現在年輕力壯。他的父親也曾是漁夫。但是骨刺會不會帶給他太多的疼痛呢？

「我不知道，」他大聲說，「我從來沒長過骨刺。」

太陽下山時，為了給自己增添自信，他想起自己在卡薩布蘭加一家酒館裡的經歷。他在那兒和一個從西恩富戈斯來的大個頭黑人比賽扳手腕，那人是碼頭上最強壯的人。整整一天一夜，他們將手肘支在桌上畫著的一條粉筆線上，小臂朝上伸直，兩人的手緊緊握在一起。兩人都試圖將對方的手壓倒在桌面上。很多人押了賭注，在煤油燈下進進出出，而他一直盯著那黑人的手臂、手，還有那黑人的臉。在過了最初八個小時之後，他們每隔四小時更換一個裁判，好讓裁判睡覺。他和黑人的指甲縫裡都滲出血來，他們倆互相瞪著對方的手、小臂，還有眼睛。下賭注的人在屋子裡走進走出，或是坐在靠牆的高腳椅上觀戰。屋裡的牆壁是木質的，都刷了鮮藍的油漆，燈光將他們的影子投射在牆壁上，那黑人的影子很龐大，當微風吹動煤油燈，他的影子就在牆上晃動著。

整個夜晚，他們的賠率反覆變來變去。那些人餵黑人喝蘭姆酒，還替他點菸。喝了蘭姆酒之後，黑人使出驚人的力氣，一度將老人的手壓下去將近三英寸。可是老人，當然那時候他還不是老人，而是冠軍聖地牙哥，又將手抬起來，將雙方拉回勢均力敵的僵局中。然後他就確信自己能夠戰勝那黑人，儘管黑人是個好人，而且是了不起的健將。天亮了，下注打賭的人都要求算作平局，裁判也直搖頭，但是他使出渾身力氣，將黑人的手一點一點往下壓，一直壓到桌面上。這場比賽是星期天早上開始的，直到星期一早上才結束。許多打賭的人要求算作平局，是因為他們還得去工作。他們要麼在碼頭上搬運麻袋裝的砂糖，要麼在哈瓦那煤礦公司上班。要不然所有人都想要看到比賽進行到底的。

75

不過，他確實結束了比賽，而且趕在大家出工之前。

在那之後好長一段時間，所有人都喊他冠軍，後來在春天的時候，又進行了一場複賽。不過大家下注的數目並不大，他相當輕鬆就贏了比賽，因為在第一次比賽時，他已經擊垮了那個來自西恩富戈斯的黑人的自信心。從那以後，他又參加過幾次比賽，之後就不再參加了。不過，他也認定，只要自己有足夠的決心，就能打敗所有人。不過，他也認定，這種比賽不利於他要用來釣魚的右手。他也曾試著用左手參加了幾次練習賽，但是他的左手總是背叛他，不會按照他的意願行事，所以他也不信任它。

這會兒太陽已快將他的左手烤好了，他想。它不會再抽筋了，除非夜裡變得太冷。誰知道今天夜裡會發生什麼事呢？

有一架飛往邁阿密的飛機從他頭頂上方飛過，他看著飛機的影子驚起了成群的飛魚。

「這兒有這麼多飛魚，就該會有鯕鰍的。」他一邊說著，一邊身體後仰著拉魚線，想看看能否將魚線再往回收一些。但他根本做不到，魚線照舊繃得緊緊的，小水珠在上面顫抖著，魚線眼看就要繃斷了。小船依然緩慢地前進著。

只要自己有足夠的決心，就能打敗所有人。

他一直盯著那架飛機看，直到再也看不見。

坐飛機的感覺一定很奇妙，他想。也不知道從那樣的高處往下看，大海會是什麼樣子？如果不是飛得太高，他們一定能清楚地看見這條大魚。我希望能在兩百英尋的高度上很慢地飛行，可以從空中俯瞰這條魚。當年在捕龜船上的時候，我曾經待在桅頂的桁桿上，即便只在那樣的高度，也能看到更多。從那兒往下看，鯕鰍的顏色似乎更綠，你還能看見他們身上的條紋和紫色斑點，他們游動時，你可以將整個魚群盡收眼底。為什麼在黑暗的深流中游得很快的魚都有紫色後背，而且通常都有紫色條紋或者紫色的斑點呢？也難怪鯕鰍在水裡看起來是綠色的，因為他本來是金黃的。可是當他們非常飢餓、需要捕食的時候，身體兩側就會出現馬林魚那樣的紫色條紋。會不會是因為憤怒、或者游得太快，他們才顯出那些條紋呢？

就在天黑之前，他們經過一個由馬尾藻堆積而成的小島，這個小島隨著波浪在海面上起伏著、搖擺著，彷彿大海在一條黃色毯子下面，正和什麼東西做愛。就在這時，他的小魚線釣住了一條鯕鰍。他第一眼看見那條鯕鰍，是在牠躍出水面的瞬間，在太陽的餘暉裡，牠顯出真正的金色。牠一次又一次跳到空

78

中，彎曲身體，拚命拍打著，就像在表演一種出於恐懼的雜技。老人想辦法讓自己回到船尾，蹲下來，用右手和右臂穩住那根粗魚線，用左手將鰍鰍往回拉，每收回一段魚線，他都用自己光著的左腳踩住。鰍鰍被拉到船尾時，絕望地來回亂竄亂跳。老人從船尾探出身去，把這條有紫色斑點而金光閃閃的魚拎上了船尾。牠的嘴巴痙攣著，急促地咬著魚鉤。牠長而扁平的身體、牠的尾巴和腦袋，都用力拍打著小船的艙底，直到老人用木棍敲擊牠金光閃耀的腦袋，才讓牠在顫抖中平靜下來。

老人把魚從魚鉤上卸下來，重新裝上一條沙丁魚做魚餌，並將魚線拋回海裡。然後他又想辦法慢慢回到船頭。他洗了洗左手，在褲子上擦乾。然後他把那根粗魚線從右手交到左手，在海水裡洗了洗右手。與此同時，他觀察著太陽沉入大海，還有那根粗魚線傾斜的角度。

「他完全沒什麼變化。」他說。但是當他觀察拍打手掌的海水時，察覺到小船的速度明顯慢了下來。

「我要把兩支船槳綁起來橫在船尾，這樣在夜裡就能減慢他的速度，」他說，「他為夜晚做好了準備，我也是。」

最好等一會兒再收拾這條鮨鰍，好讓牠的血多保留一點在肉裡，他想。我可以等一會兒再弄，到時候一併把船槳也綁好，給小船添加些阻力。眼下我最好還是讓這條魚保持平靜，日落時分可不能過分驚擾他。因為對所有的魚來說，日落是他們的艱難時刻。

他舉起手在空中晾乾，又用手抓住魚線，盡量讓自己放鬆下來，聽任自己被魚線朝前拉，直到將身體緊貼在船頭木板上。這樣，小船就承擔了一半的張力，也許還更多。

我已漸漸學會了怎麼做，他想。至少這一方面是學會了。再說他從吞下魚餌到現在，還沒吃過任何東西呢。他如此龐大的身軀，一定需要吃很多食物才行。我已經吃了一整條鮪魚。明天我會吃這條鮨鰍。他用西班牙語管這條鮨鰍叫作 dorado。也許我把牠收拾乾淨時就吃上一點。牠比鮪魚更難吃，然而，又有什麼是容易的呢？

「你現在感覺如何，魚？」他大聲問道，「我現在感覺很好，我還有夠吃一天一夜的食物，你就繼續拉著小船吧，魚。」

他並非真的感覺很好，斜勒在背上的魚線所造成的疼痛，似乎越過疼痛，進入了一種麻木的狀態，這讓他很不放心。不過他想，比這更糟的事情我都遇上過呢。我的手只是割破了一點點，另一隻手也不再抽筋了。我的兩條腿都沒問題。而在食物方面，我可是比他占了優勢啊。

現在天已經完全黑了，到了九月分，太陽一下山，天很快就黑了。他靠在船頭破舊的木板上，盡可能讓自己休息。第一簇星星出現了。他不知道獵戶星座最亮的那顆星的名字，但是一看見它，老人就知道其他星星很快就都會出現的，所有這些遙遠的朋友都會出現。

「這條魚也是我的朋友，」他大聲說，「這樣的一條魚，我真是見所未見，聞所未聞。但我又必須殺死他。幸虧我們還不必去捕殺那些星星。」

想像一下，如果人每天都必須殺死月亮，他想。月亮就會逃走。然而再想像一下，如果人每天都必須殺死太陽，又會怎樣？我們生來還算是幸運的，他想。

於是他為這條沒有東西可吃的大魚感到難過，然而要殺死他的決心，沒有因為這種難過而減弱。這魚能餵飽多少人啊，他想。可是那些人配吃他嗎？不配，當然不配。從他的行為舉止和他那偉大的尊嚴來看，沒有一個人配得上吃

81

他。

我弄不明白這些事，他想。我們無須去殺死太陽，殺死月亮或者星星，這是好事。要靠著出海打魚為生、要殺死我們真正的兄弟，已經夠糟了。

眼下，他想，我得考慮一下用船槳增添阻力的事了。這麼做有風險，也有好處。如果這條魚用盡全力往前拉，而船槳確實產生了阻力，使小船變得太過沉重的話，我有可能放出太多魚線，以致讓他逃脫。如果船的阻力小，就會延長我們雙方的痛苦，對我來說卻更加保險，因為這條魚能夠游得非常快，而他還不曾施展過這項本領呢。不過無論如何，我得把鰍鰍收拾乾淨，以免他爛掉，還要吃上一點，讓自己有力氣。

現在我要讓自己再休息一個小時，等我感覺那魚徹底平穩下來，再回船尾做這件事，還要為船槳的事做個決定。在這期間，我可以看看他如何行動、是否有什麼變化。利用船槳是個好計策；可是到了這個時候，一切都要穩紮穩打，不能冒任何風險。他依然很有活力。我看見魚鉤掛在他的嘴角上，而他緊閉著嘴巴。魚鉤帶來的折磨不算什麼。忍受飢餓的折磨，還要應付一個完全不瞭解的對手，才是他面臨的最大考驗。趕緊休息吧，老傢伙，讓他忙吧，一直忙到你來換班的時候。

他認為自己已經休息了兩個小時。月亮要到很晚才會升起，眼下他沒有辦法判斷時間。其實他並沒有真正地休息過，也許只不過稍稍放鬆了片刻。他的肩膀還在忍受著大魚的拉力，只是透過放在船頭邊緣的左手，他越來越多地依靠小船自身來抵禦這種拉力。

如果我把魚線固定在船上，事情就容易多了，他想。可是他只需一個猛衝，就有可能把魚線掙斷。我只能用自己的身體來緩衝魚線的拉力，而且隨時要準備著用雙手往外放線。

「可是你還沒有睡過覺呢，老傢伙，」他大聲地說，「已經過了半天和一整夜，現在又過了一天，你一直都沒有睡覺。如果那魚安靜又穩定，你必須想個法子讓自己睡一會兒。如果你一直不睡，腦袋就會變得不清楚。」

我的腦袋夠清楚的，他想。太清楚了。我的腦袋就像星星一樣清楚，而星星，都是我的兄弟。不過我還是要睡覺。星星會睡覺，月亮和太陽也睡覺，就連大海在那些特定的日子裡有時也睡覺，那時沒有海流的運動，大海風平浪靜。

記住，要睡覺，他想。找一個簡單又穩妥的辦法來處理魚線，然後強迫自己睡一覺。現在還是回到船尾去，處理好那條鯕鰍。如果你非得睡覺的話，把船槳橫綁在船尾來增加阻力的做法就太冒險了。

我不睡覺也可以的，他對自己說。但那樣還是太冒險了。

他用他的方式回到船尾，雙手和雙膝著地，小心翼翼，不去驚動那條魚。

也許他這會兒正半夢半醒呢，他想。我可不想讓他休息，他得一直拖著這條船，至死方休。

回到船尾後，他轉身用左手拉住勒在肩上的魚線，用右手從刀鞘裡拔出刀來。此時星光很亮，他能清楚地看見那條鯕鰍。他將刀刃扎進鯕鰍的頭部，把他從船尾下面拖出來。他一隻腳踩在魚身上，倏然一刀，從肛門一直劃到下巴。然後他放下刀子，用右手掏出魚的內臟，將魚腹裡面收拾乾淨，把魚鰓也摘掉了。他覺得魚的內臟拿在手裡沉甸甸的，滑溜溜的，於是用刀將他剖開。原來這裡面有兩條飛魚，還很新鮮緊實。他將飛魚並排放好，然後把鯕鰍的內臟和鰓從船尾丟進水中。這些東西往下沉的時候，在水中留下一道磷光。鯕鰍在星光下冷冰冰的，呈現出麻瘋病似的灰白顏色。老人用右腳踩住魚頭，剝去一側的魚皮。然後將魚翻個身,剝掉另一側的魚皮,又將兩側的魚肉由頭至尾割下來。

他把魚骨丟到船外,觀察它是否會在水裡打旋。然而只有它慢慢下沉時泛起的磷光。他轉過身來,把兩條飛魚夾在兩片魚肉中間,將刀子收回刀鞘,又用他的老辦法慢慢移向船頭。他用右手拿著魚肉,魚線的重量壓在後背上,使他的身體有些佝僂。

回到船頭,他將兩片魚肉攤在木板上,飛魚就擱在旁邊。然後,他將肩上的魚線挪了一下位置,又用放在船沿上的左手抓著。他靠在船邊,在海水裡洗飛魚,留意著海水從手上流過時的速度。因為剝過魚皮,他手上發出磷光。他觀察著手上流過的海水。水流的強度減弱了。當他在船邊的木板上摩擦手掌時,星星點點的磷光飄散開來,慢慢漂向船尾。

「他要麼是累了,要麼在休息,」老人說,「現在我得把這鯕鰍吃下去,再休息一下,或者睡一會兒。」

在越來越冷的夜晚,在星光下,他吃下半片鯕鰍肉和一條挖去內臟、切掉頭部的飛魚。

85

「如果把鯕鰍煮熟了吃，該是多麼美味，」他說，「而生吃是多麼難吃啊。

以後要不帶上鹽或者萊姆，我就不上船出海了！」

如果我有腦袋的話，整個白天就會在船頭潑上海水，讓它曬乾，就能做出些鹽來，他想。可是等我釣到這條鯕鰍時，太陽都快要下山了。不管怎麼說，就是準備得不夠。但我還是細嚼著吃下去了，而且沒有噁心想吐的感覺。

東邊天空上，雲彩越來越多，他熟悉的星星一顆接一顆消失不見。現在看起來，他好像正漂進一個雲彩的大峽谷中，而風已經停息了。

「不出三、四天，天氣就要變壞了，」他說，「但是今天夜裡不會，明天也不會。趁著那魚現在安靜又穩定，你趕緊設法睡一覺吧，老傢伙。」

他用右手緊緊握住魚線，又用大腿抵住右手，同時他將全身重量靠在船頭木板上。然後他將肩上的魚線稍稍向下移動，並用左手支撐著。

他想，只要魚線有左手支撐著，我的右手就能拉得住它。如果在我睡著的時候，魚線鬆開了，並且往外滑動，我的左手就會弄醒我。這樣右手會很辛苦。我哪怕只睡上二十分鐘或者半個小時，就很好了。

他身體前傾，蜷縮著，用全身拉住魚線，又把全身的重量壓到右手上，睡著了。

他沒有夢見獅子，卻夢見好大一群鼠海豚，他們的隊伍延伸了足有八英里或者十英里，現在正是他們的交配季節，他們會高高躍起在空中，然後落回他們跳躍時形成的水渦裡。

接著他又夢見自己回到村裡，躺在自己的床上，北風呼嘯，他感到非常冷，而且他右邊的手臂有些麻木，因為他把手臂當作枕頭，休息時，他的頭一直壓在上面。

之後，他開始夢見長長的黃色沙灘，在早早降臨的暮色中，他看到最先來到沙灘上的那頭獅子，然後其他獅子也來了。大船拋下鐵錨停泊在那兒，岸上吹來徐徐的晚風。他把下巴靠在船頭的木板上，他等著，想看看是否有更多獅子到海灘上來。他非常快樂。

月亮升起很久了，他還在睡著，那魚平穩地拉著小船，而小船進入了雲彩的隧道裡。

突然間他被驚醒了，他緊握的右手突然向上撞在他的面部，魚線飛快地從右手往外滑動，他的掌心像火燒一樣。他的左手完全失去了知覺。他竭力用右手拉住魚線，但魚線依然迅猛地向外衝去。後來他的左手終於抓住了魚線，他的背也向後頂住魚線，於是他的後背和左手像火燒一樣。他的左手由於承受了全部的張力，被傷得很厲害。他回頭看看那些備用線捲，它們正順暢地往外釋放著魚線。就在這時候，那魚跳起來，破水而出，又重重落回水中。然後他一次又一次跳出水面，儘管魚線疾速向外滑動，小船還是很快地前進著，老人拉緊魚線，幾乎到了繃斷的邊緣，而且一次又一次，他拉到了魚線的極限。他自己也被拖倒了，身體緊貼在船頭，他的臉埋在那片鯕鰍肉裡，動彈不得。

這就是我們一直在等的，他想。那我們就好好對付吧。

要讓他為魚線付出代價，他想。一定要讓他為此付出代價。

他看不到那條魚的跳躍，只聽到他衝破海面的迸裂聲，還有落下時巨大的浪花飛濺的響動。魚線以極快的速度往外滑動，嚴重傷害著他的雙手，但他早已料到會發生這樣的事情，盡量讓魚線勒在長老繭的部位，不讓它滑到掌心去，也不讓它割傷手指。

如果那個男孩在這裡，就會幫著把線捲打濕，他想。是啊，如果男孩在這裡，如果男孩在這裡。

魚線依然在往外滑，往外滑，往外滑，不過現在正在慢下來，因為那魚每

88

拖走一英寸，他都讓他付出代價。這時他從木板上抬起頭，擺脫了那片被他的臉頰壓爛的魚肉。然後他雙膝跪著，接著他慢慢地站立起來。他繼續往外放著魚線，但放得越來越慢。他設法挪動身子，雖然看不見，卻能用腳搆到那些備用的魚線。還有足夠的魚線，而現在，那魚不得不克服那些新增魚線在海水中的阻力。

幹得好，他想。那魚已經跳躍了不下十幾次，他後背的魚鰾裡現在充滿了空氣，所以他不可能再沉入海底並且死在那兒了，要是那樣，我還真沒法把他弄上來。他很快就會開始轉圈子了，我還要繼續對付他。我很好奇，是什麼讓他如此突然地開始跳躍呢？會不會是飢餓讓他鋌而走險，或者夜裡受到什麼驚嚇？也許他突然間感到恐懼了。但他是一條如此鎮定而強壯的魚，看起來似乎無所畏懼又信心十足。真是有點奇怪呢。

「你最好也無所畏懼、信心十足，老傢伙，」他說，「你重新控制了他，但還沒法收回魚線。不過他很快就要轉圈子了。」

老人用左手和雙肩拉住魚線，彎下身去，用右手抄起水來，洗去臉上粘著的被壓爛的鰍鰍肉。他怕這東西令他反胃，他可能會嘔吐，損耗自己的體力。

把臉洗乾淨之後，他靠在船邊洗右手，又把右手一直浸在海水裡，這時他注視著日出之前的第一縷光線。他幾乎是朝著正東方向，他想。這意味著他已經累了，正隨著海流往前游。很快他就要轉圈子了。那時我們真正的工作才會開始。

當他認為右手在海水裡浸得夠久了，就把手從海水裡拿出來，看了看。

「還不算太糟，」他說，「疼痛對男人來說不算什麼。」

他小心地握著魚線，不讓它嵌進那些剛被割破的新傷口裡，然後轉移一下身體的重心，這樣他就可以從小船的另一邊把左手伸進海水裡。

「你這廢物，幹得還不算太差，」他對自己的左手說，「可是有好一會兒，我根本不知道你在哪裡。」

為什麼我生來沒有兩隻好手呢？他想。也許是我自己的錯，我沒有好好訓練這隻手。可是上帝知道，它有足夠的機會去學習。不過它在夜裡幹得還不錯，而且它只抽過一回筋。要是它再抽筋的話，就讓魚線把它割斷吧。

當他這麼想的時候，他知道自己的頭腦不太清醒了，於是他認為自己應該再吃一些鯕鰍肉。但是不行，他對自己說。頭昏腦脹總比反胃要好，反胃會讓你渾身乏力。而且我知道，即使吃下去也會吐出來，因為我的臉剛剛被壓在那

90

片肉裡。只要牠不壞掉，我就留著應急吧。現在要想靠營養來增強體力已經太晚了。你真蠢，他對自己說。把另外那條飛魚吃了吧。

牠就在那兒，收拾乾淨了，隨時能吃。於是他用左手把牠撿起來，開始吃，仔細咀嚼著魚骨，將牠從頭到尾吃光了。

牠比其他所有的魚都更有營養，他想。至少能給我現在需要的力氣。現在我已經做了我能做的，讓那魚開始轉他的圈子吧，讓這場搏鬥快來吧。

從他來到海上到現在，太陽正第三次升起來，而那魚，就在此時轉起了圈子。

只憑魚線的傾斜，他還不能看出魚在轉圈。那還為時過早。他只是感覺到魚線的張力有一點點鬆弛，於是他開始用右手輕輕拉動魚線。可是魚線又像原來那樣繃緊了。當他把魚線拉得快要繃斷時，它又開始鬆動了。他將魚線從肩膀和頭頂滑下來，緩慢而平穩地收著魚線。他用雙手拉住魚線搖擺著，試圖以身體和雙腿的力氣，盡量收回魚線。他的兩條老腿和雙肩也隨著雙手的搖擺而扭動。

「這可真是一大圈，」他說，「不過他可算是轉圈了。」

這時魚線再也不能收回更多了，他依然用力拉著，直到在陽光裡看到小水珠從魚線上迸了出來。隨後魚線又開始向外滑動，老人跪下身子，很不情願地把魚線放回黑暗的海水中。

「他現在轉到圈子的外緣了。」他說。我一定要盡全力拉住魚線，他想。魚線的張力會讓他的圈子越轉越小。也許不出一個小時，我就能看見他了。現在我一定要制伏他，然後我一定要殺死他。

然而那魚一直轉著圈子，兩個小時之後，老人已是汗流浹背，渾身濕透，疲勞的感覺滲透了他的每一根骨頭。不過那魚轉的圈子現在小多了，根據魚線傾斜的角度，他看出那魚在游動時開始穩定地上浮著。

大約一個小時之前，老人眼前開始出現黑色斑點，汗水醃痛他的雙眼，醃痛眼睛上方和額頭的傷口。他倒不擔心眼前的黑色斑點，長時間這麼拉著魚線，由於過分的緊張，出現這種情況也算正常。可是已經有兩次了，他感到自己頭暈目眩，這讓他真的很擔心。

「我可不能讓自己失望，就這麼為一條魚而丟了性命。」他說，「既然我已經很漂亮地釣到如此不同凡響的大魚，求上帝保佑我堅持下去。我會念一百

92

遍天主經和一百遍聖母經。只是我現在還沒辦法念。」

就當我已經念過了吧，他想。我以後會念的。

就在這時，他感到雙手握著的魚線突然傳來劇烈的撞擊和急促的拉動。這

一次來勢很猛，非常強勁而且沉重。

那魚正用他的長嘴撞擊魚鉤和魚線之間的鋼絲，他想。這是必然要發生

的。他不得不這麼做。這也許會讓他跳起來，而我現在倒情願他接著轉圈。為

了透氣，他必須跳出水面。但是他每跳一次，魚鉤造成的傷口就會裂開得更寬

一些，最後他就有可能甩脫魚鉤。

「不要跳啊，魚，」他說，「不要跳。」

那魚又反覆多次地撞擊著鋼絲，他的頭每擺動一次，老人就只好再放出一

點魚線。

我不能再加劇他的疼痛了，他想。我的疼痛不算什麼。我能控制自己，而

他的疼痛卻能讓他發瘋。

過了一會兒，那魚不再撞擊魚鉤上的鋼絲，又開始慢慢地轉起了圈子。老

人現在正穩定地收進魚線。然而他再次感到頭暈。他用左手弄些海水上來，灑

在頭上。然後他又多灑一點水，揉擦自己的後脖頸。

「我沒有抽筋，」他說，「他很快就會浮上來，我能堅持得住。你必須堅持住，這事可沒什麼好說的。」

他靠著船頭跪了片刻之後，讓魚線重新滑到背上。趁著那魚往外轉圈的時候，我要休息一下，等他轉回來，我要站起身來好好對付他。他這樣下定了決心。

在船頭休息一下，讓那魚自己轉一圈，不用往回收魚線，這可真是個大誘惑。可是，當魚線上的張力表明那魚正轉身向小船游來的時候，他就站了起來，又開始扭動身體，擺動著雙手，將他能夠拉動的魚線盡可能地收回來。

我從來沒有這樣疲勞過，他想，而現在正吹起信風來。我正好可以借著風勢把那魚拖回來。真是幫了我的大忙啊。

「等他下次轉到遠處時，我還要休息一下，」他說，「那樣我的狀態會好很多，等他再轉上兩三圈，我就會抓住他了。」

他的草帽被推到後腦勺上，當他感覺到魚在轉身向外，就拉著魚線，在船頭坐了下去。

你先忙著吧，魚，他想。等你轉回來，我再對付你。

海上的風浪已經大了起來。不過這只是晴朗天氣裡常常出現的東北風，他只有靠風才能回家。

「我只要往南往西航行就行，」他說，「真正的男人在海上不會迷失方向，何況這是狹長的島。」

當魚轉到第三圈，他看見了他。

起初他看見那魚只是一道水下的暗影，花了好長時間從小船下面通過，而他幾乎不敢相信，那魚竟有如此的長度。

「不可能，」他說，「他不可能有這麼大。」

但他確實就是這麼大，當他轉完這一圈，在離小船只有三十碼遠的地方浮向水面，老人看見他的尾巴從水裡伸出來。那尾巴高聳在海面上，比一把長柄大鐮刀還要高，在暗藍的海水上方，呈現出很淺的淡紫色。那魚將尾巴向後斜掃一下，貼著水面游動起來。這時老人能看見他龐大的身軀，還有環繞全身的紫色條紋。他的背鰭低垂，而巨大的胸鰭寬闊地張開著。

當魚再轉一圈回來，老人就能看見他的眼睛了，還看見兩條乳臭未乾的灰

95

色小魚，正跟在大魚身邊游動。他們時而偎在大魚身上，時而又倏然游開。

有時候，他們從容地游動在大魚的陰影裡。他們每一條都有三英尺多長，當他們快速游動時，會像鰻魚一樣猛烈地甩動著身體。

老人這時汗如雨下，除了太陽曬，還有別的原因。那魚每一次平靜而沉著地轉身回來時，他都一直緊張地收著魚線。他確信，等那魚再轉兩圈，自己就有機會把魚叉扎進他的身體。

但我必須將他拉得近一些、近一些，再近一些，他想。我不應該扎他的腦袋。我必須扎他的心臟。

「你要又穩又狠，老傢伙。」他說。

又轉了一圈，那魚的背脊浮出水面了，但他離小船還是太遠了些。他又再轉了一圈，還是有些遠。不過他浮出水面更高了。於是老人確信，只要再收回一些魚線，就可以把他拖到船邊來。

他早早就準備好魚叉了，繫著魚叉的那捲細繩裝在一隻圓筐裡，繩子的另一端被牢牢拴在船頭的纜柱上。

這時那魚再一次轉了回來，平靜而優美，只有他巨大的尾巴在擺動。老人竭盡全力拉動魚線，想讓他靠得更近一些。只有短短的片刻，那魚的身體微微傾仄，然後就調整好身姿，繼續轉下一個圈子。

「我拉動他了，」老人說，「我剛剛拉動他了。」

現在他又感到頭暈了，但是他盡力拉住大魚。我剛剛拉動他了，他想。也許這一次我能把他拉過來。拉呀，我的手，他想。站穩呀，我的腿。給我堅持下去呀，我的頭。給我堅持下去。你絕不可以現在暈倒，這一次我一定要把他拉過來。

然而，當他拿出全身的力量，幾乎用上吃奶的力氣去拉動那魚時，那魚還是沒有靠到船邊來，而且那魚還沒有使出全力。大魚只不過稍稍側了一下身子，就又調整好姿態，兀自游開。

「魚啊，」老人說，「魚，無論如何你即將難免一死了。是否你也一定要殺死我呢？」

照這樣下去終究一事無成，他想。他的嘴巴已經乾得說不出話來，可是現在他搆不到裝水的瓶子。這一次我必須把他拉到船邊來，他想。我現在的狀態已經不能再應付他轉更多的圈子了。不，你能，他對自己說。你永遠都能。

在接下來的一圈，他幾乎就要把他拉過來了。然而又一次，那魚端正了身姿，緩緩游開去。

你在殺死我呀，魚，老人想。不過你有權這麼做。我從未見過比你更大更優美，或者更冷靜更高貴的生物，我的兄弟。來吧，來殺死我。我一點都不在乎誰殺死誰。

你現在頭腦糊塗了吧，他想。你必須保持頭腦清醒。保持頭腦清醒，像個男人那樣，懂得如何去受苦。或者像條魚那樣，他想道。

「清醒吧，我的頭，」他用連自己都聽不見的聲音說，「清醒吧。」

魚又轉了兩圈，一切都是老樣子。

我可能撐不住了，老人想。每一次他都覺得自己快要暈倒了。我可能不行了。但我一定要再試一次。

他又試了一次，當他已經迫使那魚轉身的時候，忽然覺得自己就要暈倒，那魚調整好姿態，又緩慢地游開了，他巨大的尾巴在空氣中擺動著。

我要再試一次，老人暗自發誓，儘管他的雙手現在已是血肉模糊，而眼前的一切彷彿在不停地閃動。

他又試了一次，還是老樣子。雖然他感覺到自己還沒動手就要暈倒了，卻想著：我還要再試一次。

他拿出自己忍受的全部疼痛，和僅存的體力，以及久已不見的驕傲，用來對付那魚的殊死掙扎。然後那魚被拉到他的身邊，在他身邊溫和地游動著，喙形魚嘴幾乎碰到小船的船板，接著又沿著小船邊游動，很長、很深、很寬，銀色身體，有紫色的條紋，在水裡似乎無窮無盡。

老人丟下魚線，用腳踩住，盡可能地將魚叉舉向高處，然後使出全部的力氣，加上他剛剛調動出來的力氣，將它扎向那魚身體的一側，就在胸鰭的後面，那胸鰭高高升起在空中，和老人的胸部一般高。他感覺到魚叉的鐵齒已經扎入魚的身體，於是他倚靠在魚叉上，想扎得更深一些，然後他將全身的重量都壓了上去。

這時那魚忽然活躍起來，儘管死亡已在他體內，他仍然從水中高高躍起，將他令人讚歎的長度和寬度，還有他的力量和美麗，完全展示出來。老人站在小船上，那魚彷彿懸掛在他頭頂上方的半空裡。然後，他轟然一聲跌入水中，猛烈撞擊所激起的浪花，噴濺到老人身上，濺滿了整條小船。

99

老人覺得頭暈和噁心，而且眼睛也看不清了。不過他還是整理好繫著魚叉的繩子，讓它從皮開肉綻的雙手間慢慢滑出去，當他能看清的時候，他看見那魚背部朝下，銀色的肚皮朝上，魚叉杆子從他肩部斜伸出來，從他心臟裡流出的鮮血把海水都染紅了，起初那血的顏色很深，就像藍色海水中超過一英里深處的一處暗礁，然後像雲彩一樣擴散開來。那魚泛著銀色光澤，一動也不動，隨波浪漂浮。

老人用他很弱的視力仔細看了看。然後他將魚叉的繩子在船頭的纜柱上繞了兩圈，用雙手托住自己的腦袋。

「要保持頭腦清醒，」他靠在船頭的木板上說道，「我是個累壞了的老傢伙，但我已經殺死了這條魚，儘管他是我的兄弟，而現在，我可要做些苦差事了。」

現在我要準備套索和繩子，好把他綁在船邊，他想。即使我有幫手，先將小船注滿水，把魚弄到船上來，再將水都舀出去，讓小船浮起，即使採用這樣的辦法，這條小船也無法裝下他。我要做好一切準備，然後把他拖過來，好好綁在船邊，然後豎起桅杆，揚起帆，返航回家。

他開始動手將那魚往船邊拉，想讓那魚靠在船邊，這樣他就可以用一根繩子穿進他的鰓，再從嘴裡抽出來，將他的腦袋緊緊綁在船頭一側。我要看看他，碰碰他，摸摸他。他是我的財產。但這不是我要摸一摸他的理由。我覺得我已經碰到他的心臟了，他想。那是我第二次用力壓向魚叉杆子的時候。現在就把他拖過來，牢牢地綁起來，用一根套索綁住他的尾巴，再用一根套索綁住他的中段，把他和小船牢牢地綁在一起。

「開始幹活吧，老傢伙。」他說，他喝了很小一口水，「戰鬥結束了，還有許多苦差事等等著你做呢。」

他抬頭望望天空，又看看那魚。他仔細看了看太陽。他想，中午才過去沒多久。而且刮起了信風。這些魚線都用不上了。等回到家裡，男孩和我會一起再將它們拼接起來。

「過來吧，魚。」他說。但是那魚並沒有過來，反而在海裡翻滾起來。老人只好把小船靠到他那兒去。

當他和那魚靠攏在一起，並讓魚頭靠著船頭時，他簡直不能相信他有這麼大。他從纜柱上解下連著魚叉的繩子，將繩子穿進魚鰓，又從魚嘴裡抽出來，

101

然後在魚的尖嘴上繞了一圈，穿進另外一側的魚鰓，在魚嘴上再繞一圈，將繩子兩端打了個結，緊緊地拴到船頭的纜柱上。他割下剩餘的繩子，走到船尾去，用繩子套住魚尾巴。那魚已經從原來的紫色和銀色變成了單一的銀白色，他身上的那些條紋，顯出和魚尾一樣的蒼白的藍紫色。那些條紋比一個人張開五指的手還寬，而那魚的眼睛，看上去不帶一絲感情，超然物外，彷彿是潛望鏡的一枚鏡片，或者是行進佇列中的聖徒。

「只能這樣殺死他，沒有別的辦法。」老人說。喝下一點水之後，他感覺好些了，他知道自己不再會暈倒，而且頭腦很清醒。看起來他至少也有一千五百磅，如果去掉頭尾和內臟，還有三分之二的淨重，按三角錢一磅來算，該是多少呢？

「我需要一支鉛筆來算一算，」他說，「我的頭腦可沒那麼清楚。不過我想，偉大的狄馬喬今天該為我感到驕傲。雖然我沒有長骨刺，但我的雙手和我的背可真是痛得厲害。」我很想知道骨刺究竟是什麼，他想。也許我們都有骨刺，只是自己沒有覺察罷了。

他將那魚緊緊地綁在船頭、船尾和中間的橫座板上。他如此之大，看起來就像小船旁邊綁了另一條大得多的船。他割下一段魚線，將魚的下巴和他的長嘴綁在一起，這樣他的嘴就不會張開了，小船行進起來就不會有額外的阻力。

然後他升起桅杆，裝上斜桁和帆腳杆，展開滿是補丁的船帆，小船開始滑行了，於是他斜躺在船尾，朝著西南方向，返航而去。

他不需要羅盤來告訴他哪裡是西南。僅憑著信風吹在身上的感覺和船帆牽引的動態，他就能辨明方向。我最好將一根細魚線掛上假餌放出去，想辦法弄些吃的，或者喝點什麼潤一潤嘴巴。但是他找不到假餌，他的沙丁魚也都腐臭了。所以當小船從黃色馬尾藻旁經過時，他用拖鉤拉上一簇來，使勁地抖動，讓海藻裡的小蝦掉落在船板上。小蝦有十多隻，他們活蹦亂跳，像沙蚤似的。

老人用拇指和食指掐掉蝦頭，連殼帶尾放進嘴裡嚼著吃了。蝦子雖然很小，但他知道這些蝦子很有營養，再說味道也不錯。

老人瓶子裡的水只夠喝兩口了，吃完蝦子，他喝了半口。如果考慮到小船極大的負荷，它現在算是行駛得很不錯了。他將舵柄夾在腋下，駕馭著小船。他看得見那條魚，而且只要他看看自己的雙手，感覺一下靠在船尾的後背，就能知道這是真實發生過的事情，不是一場夢。在事情臨近尾聲的時候，他的感

103

覺糟糕極了，那時他曾經想，也許這只是一場夢。後來他看到那魚躍出水面，在落下之前，靜止不動地懸在半空裡，才確認有奇妙的事情發生了，而他卻不敢相信。當時他的眼睛還看不清楚，雖然現在他的視力已經恢復了。

現在他知道那魚是存在的，他雙手和後背的疼痛也不是夢。他想，這雙手很快就會好的。我把傷口的壞血都放乾淨了，帶鹽的海水會治好手的。真正墨西哥灣的深色海水是這世上最了不起的良藥。我只需要讓頭腦保持清醒就好。

雙手做完了它們的工作，我們的航行也順利。那魚緊閉著嘴巴，尾巴豎得筆直，我們一起航行，像一對兄弟。這時他的腦袋又有些糊塗了，他想，是那魚正帶著我回家，還是我帶著他回家？如果我把他拖在船的後面，就不會有這種疑問了。如果那魚被我拖到這條小船上來，弄得他尊嚴掃地，那也不會有什麼疑問。

可是他們現在肩並肩地綁在一起航行著，所以老人心想，如果能讓他高興，就算是他帶著我回家吧。我不過是憑著詭計才占了上風，而他對我卻毫無惡意。

他們航行得很順利，老人將手浸泡在鹹鹹的海水裡，努力保持著清醒。雲朵堆聚得很高，上面還有很多捲雲，老人由此看出，東北風會吹上一整夜。老人一直盯著那魚，目不轉睛，好確認他是真實的。此時正是第一條鯊魚來襲擊他的一個小時之前。

鯊魚的出現並非偶然。當那一大片暗紅色魚血的雲朵下沉並擴散在一英里深的海水中，他就從水底深處上來了。他上來得如此之快，如此肆無忌憚地衝破藍色海面，出現在陽光下。然後他落回海裡，找到血腥味的蹤跡，開始沿著小船和那條魚所走的路線尾隨而來。

有時他會跟丟那氣味。但他總是又重新找回，或者僅憑著一點蛛絲馬跡，他也能快速地努力追趕過來。這是一條灰鯖鯊，他天生一副好身材，使他成為大海裡游得最快的魚類，除了雙顎，他身上的一切都很美妙。他的背部和劍魚的一樣藍，腹部是銀色的，他的皮膚既光滑又漂亮。他的身材也很像劍魚，除了快速游動時緊閉的大嘴巴。此刻他就在水面下飛快地游著，高高的背鰭切開水面，沒有一絲猶豫。在他緊閉的雙唇後面，八排牙齒全都向內傾斜。這些牙齒和多數別的鯊魚那種金字塔形的牙齒不同。牙齒的形狀就像人的手指蜷曲如鳥爪時那樣，其長度幾乎和老人的手指一樣，而且兩邊都如剃刀般鋒利。這種魚生來就可以捕食大海裡所有其他魚類，他們迅捷而強壯，全副武裝，幾乎沒有任何天敵。此刻他聞到了更加新鮮的血腥味，正加速前進，藍色背鰭切開了水面。

當老人看見他游過來的時候，就知道這是一條無所畏懼的鯊魚，只要他認準了，就沒有不敢做的事。老人準備好魚叉，將繩子繫緊，同時注視著跟上來的鯊魚。繩子有點短，因為他曾經割下一截去綁那大魚了。

老人的頭腦現在不僅清醒，還很好用。他有滿滿的決心，卻只有很少的希望。好景不長久，他想。他一邊注視著鯊魚逼近，一邊朝那大魚看了一眼。這也許還是一場夢，他想。我無法阻止他襲擊我，但也許我能幹掉他。尖牙齒的傢伙，他想，你他媽倒楣了。

鯊魚飛快地逼近船尾，當他襲擊那條魚的時候，老人看見了他張開的嘴巴和奇怪的眼睛，當他衝向那條大魚尾巴上方的部位時，牙齒發出嘎吱嘎吱的聲音。鯊魚的頭露出在水面上，他的背部也正浮出水面，老人能聽見那條大魚的皮肉被撕裂的響動，就在這一刻，老人奮力將魚叉向下扎入鯊魚的頭部，正好扎在他兩眼之間的連線和沿著鼻子一直向後的延長線相交叉的那一點上。這樣的線當然不是真的存在。只有沉重而銳利的藍色腦袋和兩隻大眼，還有嘎吱作響的兇猛推進得似乎要吞噬一切的雙顎。那交叉點正好是腦子的所在，老人朝那

兒扎了下去。他用自己血肉模糊的雙手，將一支好魚叉用盡全力扎了下去。他

扎了下去，不帶任何希望，只有決心和十足的恨意。

那鯊魚翻了個身，老人看見他的眼睛裡已經沒有了生氣，接著他又翻了個身，纏上了兩道繩子。老人知道鯊魚要死了，但是他還不肯接受這一點。他仰面躺著，尾巴不停撲打，雙顎嘎吱作響，身體劃開水面，像一條快艇那樣。他的尾巴拍打海水，激起白色的浪花。當他四分之三的身體清晰地浮出水面時，繩子繃緊了，顫抖了一下，然後啪地一聲斷了。鯊魚靜靜地在水面上躺了一會兒，老人注視著他。然後他緩慢地沉了下去。

「他吃了差不多有四十多磅。」老人大聲說。他還帶走了我的魚叉，他想，而且我的魚現在又開始流血，會引來其他鯊魚。

他不想朝那條魚再多看一眼，因為他已是殘缺不全。當那魚遭到襲擊，彷彿就是他自己遭到了襲擊。

不管怎樣我已經殺死了襲擊這條大魚的傢伙，他想。而且那是我見過的最大的灰鯖鯊。上帝知道，我還是見識過一些大鯊魚的。

太美好的事情無法長久，他想。我現在真希望這是一場夢，我從來沒有釣

107

到過這條魚，我獨自躺在鋪著舊報紙的床上。

「不過，人可不是為失敗而生，」他說，「人可以被毀滅，但不能被打敗。」

雖然我因為殺了那條魚而難過，他想。現在又趕上艱難的時候了，我甚至連魚叉都沒有。那些灰鯖鯊殘忍無比而又能力超群，既強壯又聰明。但我還是比他更聰明。也許我不是比他聰明，而是武器更好。

「別想太多，老傢伙，」他大聲說，「保持這個航向，繼續往前，來什麼就對付什麼吧。」

但我一定要想點什麼，他想。因為我已經只剩下這個了。這個，還有棒球。

我真想知道，偉大的狄馬喬會不會喜歡我那樣用魚叉扎進鯊魚的腦子？這也沒什麼了不起，他想。任何人都能做到。可是，你會不會認為我血肉模糊的雙手和你的骨刺，是可以相提並論的困難呢？我無法知道你怎麼想。我的腳後跟從來沒出過任何毛病，除了有一次游泳時，我踩到一條魟魚，腳後跟被他刺中了，整個小腿都麻痺了，而且痛得難以忍受。

「想些高興的事情吧，老傢伙，」他說，「現在每過一分鐘，你就離家更近了。你損失了四十磅魚肉，可是小船也更輕快了。」

人可以被毀滅，但不能被打敗。

他心裡早就很清楚，當小船駛進海流內部的水域，勢必發生怎樣的事情。

但是現在他卻什麼辦法都沒有。

「不對，辦法還是有的，」他大聲道，「我可以把刀子綁在船槳的槳板上。」

於是他將舵柄夾在腋下，一隻腳踩住帆索，騰出手來，辦好了這件事。

「好了，」他說，「我還是那個老傢伙。但我現在不再是手無寸鐵了。」

此時微風送爽，他航行得也很順利。他只注視著那魚的前半段，他的一部分希望似乎也回來了。

不抱希望是很傻的，他想。再說我認為不抱希望是一種罪。別去想什麼罪不罪了，他想。除了罪的事，如今還有一大堆問題呢。何況我對此也沒多少理解。

我對此沒多少理解，而且我也不認為自己真的相信這個。殺死這條魚，也許就是罪。我想應該就是，即使我這樣做是為了養活自己，還讓許多人吃上魚肉。可是如此一來，所有的事情都是罪。別再想關於罪的事。現在想這個，已經為時太晚，而且還有人專門為錢幹這個。讓他們去想吧。你生來是漁夫，如同魚生來就是魚。聖彼得是漁夫，偉大的狄馬喬的父親也是漁夫。

但是他就喜歡去想與他有關的一切事情，而且也因為他既沒有報紙可讀，也沒有無線電可聽，所以他一直在想著罪的事。你殺那條魚，並非僅僅為了養活自己，或者因為要靠賣魚換取食物，他想。你殺那條魚，還為了自己的驕傲，因為你是漁夫。他活著的時候，你愛他；他死了之後，你也愛他。如果你是愛他的，那麼殺死他就不是罪。又或者，是更大的罪？

「你想太多了，老傢伙。」他大聲說道。

不過，你殺死那條灰鯖鯊倒很享受，他想。他靠捕食活魚為生，和你一樣。他既不是食腐動物，也不像有些鯊魚那樣，只是個移動的胃囊，什麼都吃。他既漂亮又高貴，而且無所畏懼。

「我殺他是為了自衛，」老人大聲說，「而且我幹得很漂亮。」

再說，世上每一種事物都以某種方式在殺死其他的事物。釣魚這件事無疑在殺死我，同時也讓我活下來。是男孩讓我活下來的，他想。我可別太自我欺騙了。

他倚靠在船邊上，從那條魚被鯊魚咬過的地方撕下一塊肉。他放在嘴裡咀嚼著，留意著品嘗他的肉質和鮮美的滋味。魚肉既結實又汁液豐富，就像其他肉類，但是沒有充血的紅色。而且沒有一點筋。他知道這樣的肉在市場上能賣到最好的價錢。然而他無法阻擋大魚的血腥味在海水裡擴散。老人知道，最糟的時刻即將來臨。

海風的風力很穩定，只是風向比先前稍稍偏回了一些。他知道，這意味著自己不會偏離航向。老人放眼向前望去，既看不到一片帆影，也看不到任何船隻或者輪船冒出的煙。只有飛魚從他的船頭兩邊掠過，還有一小片一小片的黃色馬尾藻。他甚至看不到一隻鳥。

他繼續航行了兩個小時，靠在船尾休息著，有時會嚼一小塊大馬林魚的魚肉，想讓自己透過休息來恢復體力，而就在這時，他看見了兩條鯊魚中首先露面的那一條。

「Ay！」他大聲說。這聲驚呼難以言傳，它也許只是一種聲音，當釘子穿過一個人的雙手被釘進木頭時，也許那人會不自覺地發出那樣的聲音。

「扁頭鯊。」他大聲說。此時他已經看見，在第一條鯊魚的後面，第二條鯊魚的背鰭也浮出了水面。根據他們棕褐色的三角背鰭和尾巴掃來掃去的樣子，他認出這是有著鏟形鼻子的扁頭虎鯊。他們嗅到了血腥味，亢奮起來，有時因為餓昏了頭而跟丟了，接著又興奮地重新找到了這種氣味。不過他們始終在逼近著。

老人繫緊帆索，卡住舵柄。然後他拿起綁著刀子的那支船槳。由於他的雙手已經痛得不聽使喚，他盡可能輕柔地舉起船槳。他讓握著船槳的雙手輕輕地一張一合，好讓雙手放鬆下來。然後他一邊緊緊地握住船槳，讓雙手忍受住疼痛，而不至於因為疼痛而退縮，一邊注視著鯊魚的到來。這時，他已經可以看見他們又寬又扁的鏟形腦袋，和尖部呈白色的寬闊的胸鰭。他們是一種非常可惡的鯊魚，氣味難聞，既是食腐動物又是殺手，餓急了的時候，他們連船槳和船舵都會咬。他們是這樣一種鯊魚，會趁著海龜在水面上睡覺，咬斷人家的腿和腳蹼。如果趕上他們飢餓的時候，也會襲擊待在水裡的人，即使這人身上既沒有魚血的味道，也沒有沾上魚的黏液。

「Ay，」老人說，「扁頭鯊。快過來吧，扁頭鯊。」

他們真的來了。但是他們過來的情形和那條灰鯖鯊不同。其中一條一轉身，鑽到小船下面不見了，當他一進一退地撕扯著大魚的魚肉時，老人能感覺到小船在晃動。另外一條先是用縫隙般狹長的黃眼睛盯著老人，然後飛快地游近前來，大張著他那半圓形的上下顎，朝大魚身上已經被咬過的地方咬下去。他棕褐色的頭頂和背部有清晰的線條，指示出大腦和脊髓接合的地方，老人便用船槳上綁著的刀子由那兒插進去，又抽回來，扎進鯊魚像貓一樣的黃眼睛。鯊魚鬆開那條大魚，一邊往下滑，一邊把他臨死前咬下的魚肉吞了下去。

小船還在不停地搖晃，因為另一條鯊魚還在撕咬著大魚。老人放鬆了帆索，讓小船橫擺過來，這樣那條鯊魚便從船底下露了出來。當他一看見那條鯊魚，就從船邊探出身子，用船槳猛戳過去。他只戳在了他的肉上，但是鯊魚的皮很堅硬，刀子幾乎戳不進去。這一記重擊，不僅弄疼了他的雙手，還弄疼了他的肩。不過那鯊魚很快又浮上來，腦袋露出水面，趁他的鼻子露出水面又湊向那條大魚時，老人將船槳上的刀子垂直插入他扁平腦袋的正中心。老人抽出刀子，然後又準確地扎向同一個地方。他依舊用嘴巴咬住大魚，就像掛在大魚的身上。老人又一刀捅進他的左眼。鯊魚還是沒有鬆開嘴巴。

「這還不夠？」老人說著，將刀子由脊骨和腦子之間扎了進去。這一回很容易就扎進去了，他感覺到軟骨的斷裂。老人把船槳掉轉過來，將刀片插入鯊魚的上下顎之間，想把嘴巴撬開。他轉動刀刃，當那鯊魚終於鬆開嘴並且滑開，他說：「滾吧，小扁頭。滾到一英里深的地方去吧。去找你的朋友，或者找你老媽去吧。」

老人擦乾淨刀刃，放下船槳。然後他找到帆索，升起帆，又讓小船回到原來的航線上。

「他們吃掉了這條魚的四分之一，而且都是最好的肉，」他大聲說，「我真希望這是一場夢，我從來沒有釣到過這條魚。我對此很抱歉，魚啊。所有的事情都弄糟了。」他不再說下去，他也不想再看那條魚。他的血流乾了，由於海水沖刷，他看起來就像鏡子背面的那種銀色，但他身上的條紋還依稀可辨。

「我不該出海這麼遠，魚啊，」他說，「這對你對我都沒好處。我很抱歉，魚啊。」

算了，他對自己說。看看綁刀的繩子吧，看看繩子有沒有被弄斷。然後收拾一下你的手，因為還會來更多鯊魚。

「我真希望能有塊石頭把刀磨一磨，」檢查過綁在槳把上的刀子，老人說，「我該帶一塊石頭來的。」你該帶來的東西多著呢，他想。但是你都沒帶呀，老傢伙。現在不是去想你缺少什麼的時候，想想拿你現有的東西能夠做什麼吧。

「你給我太多忠告了，」他大聲說，「我已經煩了。」

他把舵柄夾在腋下，將雙手都浸泡在海水裡，讓小船繼續向前航行。

「上帝才知道，第二條扁頭鯊咬掉了多少魚肉，」他說，「不過我的小船倒是輕快多了。」他不願去想那條大魚殘缺不全的肚子。他知道，鯊魚每一次猛烈撕扯，都會從大魚身上撕下很多肉來，而現在，大魚留下的痕跡就像穿過大海的高速公路那麼寬廣，足以引來全部的鯊魚。

這條大魚本來夠一個人吃上整整一個冬天，他想。別再想這個了，趕緊想辦法讓你的手恢復過來，去保護剩下的那些魚肉吧。跟水裡的氣味比起來，我手上的血腥味簡直可以忽略不計。再說，我的手也沒有流太多血。傷口也沒什麼大不了。或許流點血還能讓左手不再抽筋呢。

現在我還能想些什麼呢？他想。沒有了。我什麼也別想，等著要來的鯊魚吧。我希望這真的是一場夢，他想。不過誰知道呢？說不定也能逢凶化吉。

接著來的是一條單獨行動的扁頭鯊。他來勢凶猛，像一頭奔向食槽的豬，

現在不是去想你缺少什麼的時候，想想拿你現有的東西能夠做什麼吧。

如果說一頭豬有那麼寬大的嘴巴，甚至能裝下你的腦袋。老人先讓他咬住大魚，然後用船槳上綁著的刀子朝他的腦子扎下去。但是那鯊魚翻滾著身體，猛然向後退去，刀刃突然折斷了。

老人坐定下來，掌著舵。他甚至都沒有去看那條鯊魚在水裡慢慢下沉的情景，起初是真實的尺寸，然後變小，最後只剩一小點。這種情景總會吸引老人的。但是現在，他看都沒看一眼。

「現在我還有那把拖鉤，」他說，「可是那不太管用。我還有兩支船槳，一根舵柄和一根短棍。」

現在他們已經打敗我了，他想。我太老了，沒法用短棍打死鯊魚了。但是只要我還有船槳，還有短棍和舵柄，我就敢於一試。

他再次將雙手放到水裡浸泡著。現在已是午後向晚的時候了，他的視野中什麼都沒有，只有大海和天空。風比原先更大了，他希望很快就能看見陸地。

「你累了，老傢伙，」他說，「你心裡也累壞了。」

鯊魚沒有再來襲擊他，直到日落之前。

老人看見那些棕褐色的鯊魚鰭沿著大魚在水中留下的寬廣痕跡追了過來。

他們甚至無須來回搜索大魚的血腥味，肩並肩徑直撲向了小船。

他卡住舵柄，繫緊帆索，伸手到船尾下面拿出短棍。這原來是槳把，從一支斷槳上鋸下來的，長度只有兩英尺半。因為太短，他只能單手持棍。於是他將棍子拿在右手，緊緊地攥著，注視著游過來的鯊魚。來的這兩條都是扁頭鯊。

我要等第一條鯊魚緊緊咬住大魚之後，擊打他的鼻頭，或者直接打他的頭頂，他想。

兩條鯊魚同時逼近，當他看見離他最近的那一條張開雙顎，一頭拱進大魚銀色的腹部，就高舉短棍，重重地猛擊他寬寬的頭頂。棍子落下時，他感覺像是砸在了堅韌厚重的東西上。不過他也感覺到鯊魚堅硬的骨頭。當鯊魚從那條大魚身上滑落時，他又用力擊打了他的鼻頭。

另一條鯊魚一直在大魚身上進進出出地忙著，這時他又一次大張著嘴巴，老人看見白花花的魚肉從他的嘴角溢了出來。老人掄起棍子朝他打過去，只打中他的頭，鯊魚一邊看著他，一邊還把咬著的魚肉撕下來。趁他滑開去吞吃嘴裡的魚肉，老人又掄起棍子打過去，卻只打中了如橡膠般極其堅韌的地方。

「來啊，扁頭鯊，」老人說，「再過來呀。」

那鯊魚猛衝過來，趁他咬住大魚時，老人再次擊打。他將棍子盡力舉到高處，結結實實打中了他。這一次，他感覺到鯊魚腦子底部的骨頭。他又照著同樣的地方打了一棍，那鯊魚慢吞吞撕下一塊魚肉，從大魚身上滑了下去。

老人注視著，以防他再來，但是兩條鯊魚都沒有出現。然後他看見其中一條在海面上轉著圈子。他沒有看見另一條的背鰭。

我已經不指望自己能夠殺死這兩條魚了，他想。要是在當年，我能辦得到。但是我把他們兩個都傷得不輕，無論其中哪一條都不會太好受。如果我是用雙手掄著一根棒球棍，我一定已經幹掉第一條了。哪怕是現在也能做到，他想。

他不願去看那條大魚。他知道，大魚的一半已經被毀掉了。就在他和兩條鯊魚搏鬥的時候，太陽已經落下去了。

「天很快就要黑了，」他說，「很快我就能看見哈瓦那的燈火了。如果我往東偏得太遠，我就會看見一處新開海灘上的亮光。」

現在我離陸地應該不會太遠了，他想。我希望沒有人太為我擔心。當然，也只有那男孩會擔心著我。但我相信，他對我有信心。許多老漁夫會擔心我。

還有很多其他人，他想。我住在一個很善良的小鎮。

他不能和那條大魚說話了，因為他已經被摧殘得不成樣子。這時，一個念頭浮現在他的腦海裡。

「半身魚，」他說，「你曾是完整的魚呀。我悔不該出海這麼遠。我把我們兩個都毀了。但是我們殺死了很多條鯊魚，你和我，還讓另外一些半死不活了。你又曾經殺死過多少生命呢，我的老魚？你頭上那根長矛似的傢伙，也不是白長的。」

他喜歡去想像那條魚，當他還在大海裡暢游時，會怎樣對付一條鯊魚呢。我該把他長矛似的尖嘴砍下來拿著，去和那些鯊魚搏鬥，他想。可是船上沒有斧子，甚至刀也沒了。

假如我取下他的尖嘴，就可以綁在船槳上，該是多好的武器。這樣一來，我們或許能一起戰鬥。而現在，要是在夜裡鯊魚群來了，你該怎麼辦？你又能怎麼辦？

「跟他們鬥，」他說，「跟他們鬥到死。」

但是如今身處黑暗，燈火沒有出現，也看不到任何亮光，只有風，只有船

121

帆穩定的牽引，他覺得自己也許已經死了。他合攏雙手，觸摸著掌心。這雙手還沒死，只要把雙手簡單地張開又合攏，他就能領受生命之痛。他將後背靠向船尾，就知道自己還沒有死。他的肩膀也分明告訴他這一點。

他想，我曾經許願說，如果抓到了這條大魚，就要把那些祈禱文都念過。

可是我現在太累了，念不動了。我最好還是把麻袋拿過來披在肩上吧。

他躺在船尾，一邊掌著舵，一邊眺望著，期待著天空中出現燈火的微光。

我只有那魚的一半了，他想。要是運氣好，也許我能把魚的前半段帶回去。我多少總該有點好運氣吧。不，沒了，他說。你出海太遠，把你的好運氣給得罪了。

「別傻了，」他大聲道，「保持清醒，掌好舵。你的好運氣也許還多著呢。」

「如果有什麼地方出售好運氣，我倒想買它一些。」他說。

我能用什麼去買呢？他問自己。一杆失去了的魚叉、一把折斷的刀子，還有兩隻破破爛爛的手，我能用這些去買嗎？

「也許能，」他說，「你曾經想用在海上的八十四天去買，而且你幾乎就買成了。」

不要再想這些無意義的東西了，他想。所謂好運氣，它來臨的方式多種多樣，誰又能把它辨認出來呢？但是不管什麼方式的好運氣，我都想買一點，無論要付出什麼代價。我希望我能看到燈火的亮光，他想。我的願望太多了。但現在我只有這一個願望。他想辦法讓自己靠得更舒服、更方便駕馭小船，身上的疼痛告訴他，他沒有死。

大約是在夜裡的十點鐘左右，他看見了城市燈火反射過來的亮光。一開始那亮光只是依稀可見，彷彿月亮升起之前，天空顯露的微光。然後，亮光越來越穩定而清晰，雖然這時東北風漸漸增強，大海已是波濤洶湧。他將小船朝亮光裡駛去，他想著，用不了多久，他就會碰上灣流的邊緣了。

現在一切都結束了，他想。他們或許還會來襲擊我。但是一個人手無寸鐵，在這茫茫黑夜，如何抵抗呢？

此刻，他全身僵硬而酸痛，他身上的傷口，還有那些疲憊不堪的部位，在夜晚的寒氣裡，讓他疼痛難忍。我希望自己不用再鬥下去，他想。我多麼希望不用再鬥了。

然而到了午夜時分，他又開始搏鬥了，而且這一次他知道，搏鬥已無意義。

他們成群結隊而來，他只能看見他們的鰭在海面上劃出的水線，還有他們猛力撲向大魚時閃射的磷光。他不停擊打他們的頭部，他聽見他們雙顎咬咬的聲音、小船不斷搖晃的聲音，他知道那些鯊魚在小船下面，死死咬住大魚不放。

他不顧一切地掄起短棍，凡是他感覺到或是聽到的東西，都猛打一氣。他感覺到棍子被什麼抓住了，接著就被拉走了。

他用力將舵柄從船舵上抽下來，雙手緊握，用它又砸又砍，一次又一次揮舞著擊打下去。可是鯊魚已經游向船頭，一條接一條，或是同時撲上來，從大魚身上扯下一塊又一塊的肉，那些肉在海水下面閃動著白色微光，接著群鯊轉回身，重新撲過來。

終於，有一條鯊魚獨自奔向了魚頭，他明白，一切已然結束。當鯊魚的雙顎卡在沉重的魚頭裡，無法扯脫出來時，他揮起舵柄，一次又一次，朝鯊魚的腦袋打去。他聽到舵柄斷裂的聲音，於是他用斷裂的一頭向著鯊魚猛刺過去。他感覺到它扎進去了，他明白斷裂的那一頭很鋒利，於是他再次扎了進去。鯊魚鬆了嘴，翻滾開去。他是這群鯊魚中來得最晚的。這兒再也沒有什麼可吃的了。

老人現在幾乎喘不上氣來，他覺得嘴巴裡有一種奇怪的味道，帶著銅腥氣，甜絲絲的，這讓他一時有些擔心。好在這味道不算太嚴重。

他向海裡唾了一口，說道：「吃吧，扁頭鯊。去做個白日夢，妄想你們已經幹掉了這個人吧。」

他知道自己終於被打敗，沒有任何補救的餘地了，所以他回到船尾，發現殘缺的舵柄還能插進舵孔裡，還能讓他勉強地掌起舵來。他整理好圍在肩上的麻袋，讓小船順著航線繼續行駛。此時他的航行變得輕快了，他再也沒有任何想法，甚至沒有任何感覺了。他似乎超脫於所有的一切，他只是盡可能明智地將小船平安駛向回家的港口。夜裡，有幾條鯊魚又來襲擊大魚的骨骸，就像有些人從餐桌上撿食麵包屑一樣。老人對這些鯊魚毫不理會，對所有的事情毫不理會，一心掌著舵。他只留意到，現在小船行駛得有多輕快，有多令人滿意，因為船邊再也沒有沉重的負荷了。

它很好，他想。它幾乎完好無損，除了那根舵柄，它沒有受到任何損傷，而舵柄很輕鬆就可以換掉。

這時他能感覺到自己已然越過海流邊緣，來到海流的內側了，他能看見沿

125

岸分布的海濱住宅區的燈光。他瞭解自己所在的位置，回家已非難事。

無論如何，風是我們的朋友，他想。接著他補充道，有時候是。還有大海，那裡既有我們的朋友，也有我們的敵人。還有床，他想。床是我的朋友。只要一張床，他想。床是了不起的東西。當你被打敗的時候，床讓你舒服。我還從來都不知道，它有多舒服。可是，是什麼打敗了你呢，他想。

「沒什麼，」他大聲道，「我自己去得太遠了。」

當他駛入小港，露臺酒吧的燈光已經熄滅了，他知道，所有人都已經上床睡覺了。東北風不斷增強著，這會兒已經刮得很猛了。港灣裡卻是靜悄悄的，他將小船靠到礁岩下一處有鵝卵石的地方。沒有人幫忙，他只能盡力將小船靠上去。然後他走下船來，將船牢牢地拴在一塊岩石上。

他拔下桅杆，把帆捲起來，紮好。然後他扛起桅杆，向岸上爬去。現在他才知道自己有多累。他駐足片刻，回頭看去，在街燈反射過來的光線下，他看見那條大魚的尾巴，壯觀地豎立在小船的船尾後面。他看見那魚的脊骨像一條裸露的白線，還有黑暗一團的頭部和向前伸出的細長尖嘴，而在頭尾之間，那魚已是空無一物。

他看見那魚的脊骨像一條裸露的白線，還有黑暗一團的頭部和向前伸出的細長的尖嘴。

他又開始往上爬去，爬到高處時，他跌倒了，就那樣肩上扛著桅杆，在地上躺了一會兒。他努力要站起來，可是太難了。於是他肩上扛著桅杆，坐在那兒，兩眼望著大路。一隻貓從路的另一邊走過，去忙牠自己的事情。老人注視著牠走遠。然後他就只是望著大路。

終於，他放下桅杆，站起來。然後又舉起桅杆，扛在肩膀上，開始沿著大路走去。走到他的小屋之前，他不得不坐下來，歇了五次。

走進小屋，他將桅杆靠牆放下。黑暗中他找到一隻裝水的瓶子，喝了一口。然後他就躺倒在床上。他拉過毯子來，蓋住雙肩，蓋住後背和雙腿，俯身睡在那些舊報紙上，他的雙臂直直地向前伸出，而他的雙手，掌心朝天。

直到翌日的早上，男孩往門裡張望的時候，他還熟睡著。因為風刮得太猛，那些依賴風力航行的漁船都不能出海了，所以男孩睡了個懶覺，然後像每天早上那樣，起床後就到老人的小屋來探望一下。男孩看見老人還在呼吸，然後又看看他的雙手，就哭了起來。他悄悄地走出來，去給老人拿點咖啡，當他沿著大路走下去，一路上都在哭。

許多漁夫正圍著老人的小船，察看船邊綁著的東西，其中一名漁夫捲著褲腿，站在水裡，用魚線測量那副骨架的長度。

男孩沒有走過去。他剛才已經去過了，其中一個漁夫正在那兒替他看守著這條小船。

「他怎麼樣了？」一名漁夫大聲喊道。

「睡著呢，」男孩也喊著回答，他一點也不在乎別人看見他在哭，「誰都別去打擾他。」

「從鼻子到尾巴，他有十八英尺哪！」那個測量的漁夫喊道。

「我相信。」男孩說。

他走進露臺酒吧，要了一罐咖啡。

「要熱一點，再多放些牛奶和糖。」

「還要點別的嗎？」

「不要了。待會兒我看看他能吃些什麼。」

「那是好大一條魚啊，」老闆說，「從來沒見過這麼大的魚。你昨天釣的那兩條也是好魚呢。」

「狗屁我的魚呢。」男孩說著又哭了起來。

129

「你要不要喝點什麼？」老闆問道。

「不了，」男孩說，「叫他們別去打擾聖地牙哥。我等會兒再來。」

「跟他說我有多麼替他遺憾。」

「謝謝。」男孩說。

男孩拿著一罐滾熱的咖啡走回老人的小屋，在老人身邊坐下，等他醒來。

有一次，他看起來彷彿就要醒了。但是他又沉沉睡去，男孩就穿過大路，到對面借了些柴火，將咖啡重新加熱。

終於，老人醒了。

「別起身，」男孩說，「先喝點這個。」他往一隻玻璃杯裡倒了些咖啡。

老人接過咖啡，喝了下去。

「他們把我打敗了，馬諾林，」他說，「他們真的把我打敗了。」

「他沒有打敗你。那魚沒有。」

「他沒有。那倒是。那是之後發生的。」

「佩德里科在顧著小船，還有船上的東西。你想怎麼處置那魚頭呢？」

「讓佩德里科把它砍下來做魚餌吧。」

「還有那根標槍似的魚嘴呢？」

「你想要，就拿去吧。」

「我當然想要，」男孩說，「可是現在我們得安排一下別的事情。」

「他們找過我嗎？」

「當然。海岸警衛隊和飛機都出動了。」

「海太大，而船太小，很難看得見。」老人說。他發覺，能有個人說話，而不是只對自己或者只對著大海說話，是多麼讓人高興。「我很想念你，」他說，「你們釣到了什麼？」

「第一天一條，第二天一條，第三天兩條。」

「真不錯。」

「我們又可以一起釣魚了。」

「不行。我運氣不好。我不再有好運氣了。」

「去他的好運吧，」男孩說，「我會給你帶來好運的。」

「你家裡人會怎麼說？」

「我不在乎。昨天我已經釣到兩條了。現在我們可以一起釣魚了，我要向

131

你請教的事情還多著呢。」

「我們一定要弄一支鋒利的魚矛，一直放在船上。你可以弄一塊舊福特的彈簧片做矛頭。我們把矛拿到瓜納巴科亞去打磨。如果磨得太鋒利，又沒有回火加工的話，就容易折斷。我的刀子就斷掉了。」

「我會去找一把刀子來，把彈簧片也磨好。這大風還要刮幾天？」

「也許要三天，也許更久。」

「我會把一切都安排好，」男孩說，「你先把手上的傷養好，老爹。」

「我知道怎樣照顧這些傷口。夜裡我吐了一些奇怪的東西，好像胸腔裡有什麼東西碎掉了。」

「也把那兒養好，」男孩說，「躺下來吧，老爹，我去給你拿件乾淨的襯衫，再帶點吃的來。」

「順便帶幾張我不在時的報紙來。」老人說。

「你可一定要趕快好起來，我還有好多東西要向你學呢，你可以教我所有的事。你到底吃了多少苦啊？」

「夠多了。」老人說。

「我去拿報紙和吃的東西，」男孩說，「好好休息，老爹。我會到藥房去拿些藥來，幫你的手包紮一下。」

「別忘了告訴佩德里科，那魚頭給他了。」

「好的，我會記住的。」

當男孩走到門外，沿著那條破舊的珊瑚石路走去時，他又一次哭起來。

那天下午，露臺酒吧來了一群遊客，其中有個女人從一堆空啤酒罐和死梭子魚之間朝下面的海水望去，她看見一條又粗又長的白色脊骨，末端連著一個巨大的尾巴，當強勁的東風在港灣的入口外面不斷掀起大浪，那尾巴就隨著潮水起伏搖擺。

「那是什麼呀？」她指著那條大魚留下的長長的脊骨，問一名侍者。那脊骨如今只不過是垃圾，等著被潮水帶走。

「Tiburon（鯊魚），」侍者說，「哎鯊魚。」他本來是想解釋一下事情發生的經過。

「哦，我還從來都不知道鯊魚會有這麼氣派、造型這麼優美的尾巴呢。」

「我也不知道啊。」她的男伴說。

133

路那頭，在他小屋裡，老人又睡著了。他照舊是臉朝下俯臥著，男孩坐在他旁邊守候。此時老人正夢見那些獅子。

譯後記

雖然本科讀的是外文系，此前卻沒有完整翻譯過任何書籍。二十多歲年輕氣盛的時候，曾發願，不翻譯別人的作品，要讓別人來翻譯我的。其中潛臺詞，無非是我寫的作品不會比他們差，也許還比他們好，憑什麼讓我做這種「再創作」的二手工作。這樣的想法，當然是一種偏見。現在譯了這本書，算是對得起外文系的出身了。

這本書，我學生時代就讀過。其中的內容，現在幾乎成了讀書界無人不知的民間故事；硬漢的口號，也像汽車尾氣一樣，遍布城鄉，令人生厭。要不是「作家榜」用了一年多時間來說服我，並且最終打動我，即使讓我重新拿起這本書，或許都難。更不用說一字一句去翻譯了。然而，聽人勸、吃飽飯，當我拿起這本書的早期原版，譯到五分之一時，驚訝地發現，這件事做對了。在一間鬧哄哄的路邊飯館裡著著上菜，我讀著書中的一些句子，幾乎熱淚盈眶。

這是怎麼回事？難道以前我是個傻子嗎？這樣一部傑作，我竟然活生生放

137

棄了。我竟然沒有嚼出它的汁液，沒有嘗到它的美味，就隨意吐出去。誰敗了我的胃口，讓我對海明威誤解了三十年？

一部傑作在轉譯過程中，變得平庸累贅、破碎支離，其中的韻律不見蹤影，作者的良苦用心，變成了一團糾結的亂麻；那些講解和分析、那些國內外的評價和吹噓，又讓一部傑作變成了被弱智化的主題、被抽筋扒皮的殘骸。可憐的海明威、可憐的書，就像書裡寫到的那條大魚，只剩下成為垃圾的脊骨，等著被潮水帶走。

一個作家，無論他用什麼語言寫作，若能寫出一部人類之書，就是莫大的榮耀。海明威狼奔豕突一生，這本書是他留下的絕唱。其中的意象和語言，精密而結實，壯闊而哀傷。這本書和其他真正的傑作一樣，以一喻萬，言之不能盡，思之不能竭。所謂真正的傑作，幾乎就是這樣一種物質，不能被分解，不能被改造，不能被提煉。它必須整體呈現，如同那條大魚，牠的上浮過程幾乎無休無止，水流從牠身體兩側傾瀉而下。

我不是專職譯者。我可能只譯這一本。種種機緣巧合，促成了這件事。我想按照我自己的理解，把這件事做好。

我希望作品的中文譯文，不再是原作的中文說明書，換言之，它本身的文字應該就是一部傑作該有的文字。所以我用很笨的方式檢驗它。連續三週，共計九堂課，我讓學生在沒有預先準備的情況下，當眾接力朗讀。聽眾約有十數人，分屬幾個不同專業和年級。在整個朗讀過程中，每一位聽眾，包括我在內，只要對譯文的意思或聽覺感受有疑問，即可隨時叫停，提出修改的建議。我想讓在場每一個人，「用聽覺去看懂」作品的每個句子。做到了。

《老人與海》的故事發生在古巴，當地語言為西班牙語，作者在行文中不止一處使用了西班牙語詞彙，並未另行加注。

為尊重原著風貌，譯文保留其中部分詞彙，並加括弧標明詞義。我希望這部小體量的傑作，在閱讀中不被注釋的記號擾亂節奏。連綿起伏的詩意，是它行文的基本特徵。

有人問，翻譯這本書的時候，有沒有夢見海明威，他和你交談時還用英語嗎？我說夢見過，記不清他說的是英語或是中文。我說，好在一九六一年之後，他已經突破了人的局限，說不定還懂得了所有的語言，深奧難學的中文，對他來說也不再是障礙吧。

還有人問，你的譯文怎樣？算不算好？我真想這麼回答：如果海明威同學用中文寫，語感未必好過這譯文。這麼說，太狂傲。那就學著謙卑些吧，老人說，這不丟臉，也無損於真正的驕傲。「如果海明威用中文寫作，我想知道這部作品到底會是什麼樣子。」這麼說，就好多了。

既經我手，必有我氣息。努力抑制這氣息，讓它不要太重，不至於遮蔽了原作的面目和氣息，是我在翻譯過程中著力克服的困難。

我希望對得起這本書的作者，用這種費力不討好的方式感謝他。我想說，雖然錯誤在所難免，我做得還不錯。

致謝（不按筆劃順序）：

王立沙、邢若曦、谷小雨、Eric Abrahamsen，二〇一六年秋季學期選修寫作訓練 II 的同學以及前來旁聽該課程的同學。謝謝各位在這件事上對我的幫助和鼓舞。

於南京東郊

魯羊

一九六三年生於江蘇海安，著名作家、詩人，中國當代先鋒小說標桿人物。《老人與海》是他首次翻譯的完整作品，出版前，譯稿曾經國內外多方傳閱，贏得好評與讚歎，被譽為里程碑式的經典中文譯本。

"Tiburon," the waiter said. "Eshark." He was meaning to explain what had happened.

"I didn't know sharks had such handsome, beautifully formed tails."

"I didn't either," her male companion said.

Up the road, in his shack, the old man was sleeping again. He was still sleeping on his face and the boy was sitting by him watching him. The old man was dreaming about the lions.

"I will have everything in order," the boy said. "You get your hands well old man."

"I know how to care for them. In the night I spat something strange and felt something in my chest was broken."

"Get that well too," the boy said. "Lie down, old man, and I will bring you your clean shirt. And something to eat."

"Bring any of the papers of the time that I was gone," the old man said.

"You must get well fast for there is much that I can learn and you can teach me everything. How much did you suffer?"

"Plenty," the old man said.

"I'll bring the food and the papers," the boy said. "Rest well, old man. I will bring stuff from the drugstore for your hands."

"Don't forget to tell Pedrico the head is his."

"No. I will remember."

As the boy went out the door and down the worn coral rock road he was crying again.

That afternoon there was a party of tourists at the Terrace and looking down in the water among the empty beer cans and dead barracudas a woman saw a great long white spine with a huge tail at the end that lifted and swung with the tide while the east wind blew a heavy steady sea outside the entrance to the harbour.

"What's that?" she asked a waiter and pointed to the long backbone of the great fish that was now just garbage waiting to go out with the tide.

"I want it," the boy said. "Now we must make our plans about the other things."

"Did they search for me?"

"Of course. With coast guard and with planes."

"The ocean is very big and a skiff is small and hard to see," the old man said. He noticed how pleasant it was to have someone to talk to instead of speaking only to himself and to the sea. "I missed you," he said. "What did you catch?"

"One the first day. One the second and two the third."

"Very good."

"Now we fish together again."

"No. I am not lucky. I am not lucky anymore."

"The hell with luck," the boy said. "I'll bring the luck with me."

"What will your family say?"

"I do not care. I caught two yesterday. But we will fish together now for I still have much to learn."

"We must get a good killing lance and always have it on board. You can make the blade from a spring leaf from an old Ford. We can grind it in Guanabacoa. It should be sharp and not tempered so it will break. My knife broke."

"I'll get another knife and have the spring ground. How many days of heavy *brisa* have we?"

"Maybe three. Maybe more."

fish. Those were two fine fish you took yesterday too."

"Damn my fish," the boy said and he started to cry again.

"Do you want a drink of any kind?" the proprietor asked.

"No," the boy said. "Tell them not to bother Santiago. I'll be back."

"Tell him how sorry I am."

"Thanks," the boy said.

The boy carried the hot can of coffee up to the old man's shack and sat by him until he woke. Once it looked as though he were waking. But he had gone back into heavy sleep and the boy had gone across the road to borrow some wood to heat the coffee.

Finally the old man woke.

"Don't sit up," the boy said. "Drink this." He poured some of the coffee in a glass.

The old man took it and drank it.

"They beat me, Manolin," he said. "They truly beat me."

"*He* didn't beat you. Not the fish."

"No. Truly. It was afterwards."

"Pedrico is looking after the skiff and the gear. What do you want done with the head?"

"Let Pedrico chop it up to use in fish traps."

"And the spear?"

"You keep it if you want it."

palms of his hands up.

He was asleep when the boy looked in the door in the morning. It was blowing so hard that the drifting-boats would not be going out and the boy had slept late and then come to the old man's shack as he had come each morning. The boy saw that the old man was breathing and then he saw the old man's hands and he started to cry. He went out very quietly to go to bring some coffee and all the way down the road he was crying.

Many fishermen were around the skiff looking at what was lashed beside it and one was in the water, his trousers rolled up, measuring the skeleton with a length of line.

The boy did not go down. He had been there before and one of the fishermen was looking after the skiff for him.

"How is he?" one of the fishermen shouted.

"Sleeping," the boy called. He did not care that they saw him crying. "Let no one disturb him."

"He was eighteen feet from nose to tail," the fisherman who was measuring him called.

"I believe it," the boy said.

He went into the Terrace and asked for a can of coffee.

"Hot and with plenty of milk and sugar in it."

"Anything more?"

"No. Afterwards I will see what he can eat."

"What a fish it was," the proprietor said. "There has never been such a

"Nothing," he said aloud. "I went out too far."

When he sailed into the little harbour the lights of the Terrace were out and he knew everyone was in bed. The breeze had risen steadily and was blowing strongly now. It was quiet in the harbour though and he sailed up onto the little patch of shingle below the rocks. There was no one to help him so he pulled the boat up as far as he could. Then he stepped out and made her fast to a rock.

He unstepped the mast and furled the sail and tied it. Then he shouldered the mast and started to climb. It was then he knew the depth of his tiredness. He stopped for a moment and looked back and saw in the reflection from the street light the great tail of the fish standing up well behind the skiff's stern. He saw the white naked line of his backbone and the dark mass of the head with the projecting bill and all the nakedness between.

He started to climb again and at the top he fell and lay for some time with the mast across his shoulder. He tried to get up. But it was too difficult and he sat there with the mast on his shoulder and looked at the road. A cat passed on the far side going about its business and the old man watched it. Then he just watched the road.

Finally he put the mast down and stood up. He picked the mast up and put it on his shoulder and started up the road. He had to sit down five times before he reached his shack.

Inside the shack he leaned the mast against the wall. In the dark he found a water bottle and took a drink. Then he lay down on the bed. He pulled the blanket over his shoulders and then over his back and legs and he slept face down on the newspapers with his arms out straight and the

The old man could hardly breathe now and he felt a strange taste in his mouth. It was coppery and sweet and he was afraid of it for a moment. But there was not much of it.

He spat into the ocean and said, "Eat that, *galanos*. And make a dream you've killed a man."

He knew he was beaten now finally and without remedy and he went back to the stern and found the jagged end of the tiller would fit in the slot of the rudder well enough for him to steer. He settled the sack around his shoulders and put the skiff on her course. He sailed lightly now and he had no thoughts nor any feelings of any kind. He was past everything now and he sailed the skiff to make his home port as well and as intelligently as he could. In the night sharks hit the carcass as someone might pick up crumbs from the table. The old man paid no attention to them and did not pay any attention to anything except steering. He only noticed how lightly and how well the skiff sailed now there was no great weight beside her.

She's good, he thought. She is sound and not harmed in any way except for the tiller. That is easily replaced.

He could feel he was inside the current now and he could see the lights of the beach colonies along the shore. He knew where he was now and it was nothing to get home.

The wind is our friend, anyway, he thought. Then he added, sometimes. And the great sea with our friends and our enemies. And bed, he thought. Bed is my friend. Just bed, he thought. Bed will be a great thing. It is easy when you are beaten, he thought. I never knew how easy it was. And what beat you, he thought.

He steered inside of the glow and he thought that now, soon, he must hit the edge of the stream.

Now it is over, he thought. They will probably hit me again. But what can a man do against them in the dark without a weapon?

He was stiff and sore now and his wounds and all of the strained parts of his body hurt with the cold of the night. I hope I do not have to fight again, he thought. I hope so much I do not have to fight again.

But by midnight he fought and this time he knew the fight was useless. They came in a pack and he could only see the lines in the water that their fins made and their phosphorescence as they threw themselves on the fish. He clubbed at heads and heard the jaws chop and the shaking of the skiff as they took hold below. He clubbed desperately at what he could only feel and hear and he felt something seize the club and it was gone.

He jerked the tiller free from the rudder and beat and chopped with it, holding it in both hands and driving it down again and again. But they were up to the bow now and driving in one after the other and together, tearing off the pieces of meat that showed glowing below the sea as they turned to come once more.

One came, finally, against the head itself and he knew that it was over. He swung the tiller across the shark's head where the jaws were caught in the heaviness of the fish's head which would not tear. He swung it once and twice and again. He heard the tiller break and he lunged at the shark with the splintered butt. He felt it go in and knowing it was sharp he drove it in again. The shark let go and rolled away. That was the last shark of the pack that came. There was nothing more for them to eat.

His shoulders told him.

I have all those prayers I promised if I caught the fish, he thought. But I am too tired to say them now. I better get the sack and put it over my shoulders.

He lay in the stern and steered and watched for the glow to come in the sky. I have half of him, he thought. Maybe I'll have the luck to bring the forward half in. I should have some luck. No, he said. You violated your luck when you went too far outside.

"Don't be silly," he said aloud. "And keep awake and steer. You may have much luck yet."

"I'd like to buy some if there's any place they sell it," he said.

What could I buy it with? he asked himself. Could I buy it with a lost harpoon and a broken knife and two bad hands?

"You might," he said. "You tried to buy it with eighty-four days at sea. They nearly sold it to you too."

I must not think nonsense, he thought. Luck is a thing that comes in many forms and who can recognize her? I would take some though in any form and pay what they asked. I wish I could see the glow from the lights, he thought. I wish too many things. But that is the thing I wish for now. He tried to settle more comfortably to steer and from his pain he knew he was not dead.

He saw the reflected glare of the lights of the city at what must have been around ten o'clock at night. They were only perceptible at first as the light is in the sky before the moon rises. Then they were steady to see across the ocean which was rough now with the increasing breeze.

"It will be dark soon," he said. "Then I should see the glow of Havana. If I am too far to the eastward I will see the lights of one of the new beaches."

I cannot be too far out now, he thought. I hope no one has been too worried. There is only the boy to worry, of course. But I am sure he would have confidence. Many of the older fishermen will worry. Many others too, he thought. I live in a good town.

He could not talk to the fish anymore because the fish had been ruined too badly. Then something came into his head.

"Half fish," he said. "Fish that you were. I am sorry that I went too far out. I ruined us both. But we have killed many sharks, you and I, and ruined many others. How many did you ever kill, old fish? You do not have that spear on your head for nothing."

He liked to think of the fish and what he could do to a shark if he were swimming free. I should have chopped the bill off to fight them with, he thought. But there was no hatchet and then there was no knife.

But if I had, and could have lashed it to an oar butt, what a weapon. Then we might have fought them together. What will you do now if they come in the night? What can you do?

"Fight them," he said. "I'll fight them until I die."

But in the dark now and no glow showing and no lights and only the wind and the steady pull of the sail he felt that perhaps he was already dead. He put his two hands together and felt the palms. They were not dead and he could bring the pain of life by simply opening and closing them. He leaned his back against the stern and knew he was not dead.

broad head. He felt the rubbery solidity as the club came down. But he felt the rigidity of bone too and he struck the shark once more hard across the point of the nose as he slid down from the fish.

The other shark had been in and out and now came in again with his jaws wide. The old man could see pieces of the meat of the fish spilling white from the corner of his jaws as he bumped the fish and closed his jaws. He swung at him and hit only the head and the shark looked at him and wrenched the meat loose. The old man swung the club down on him again as he slipped away to swallow and hit only the heavy solid rubberiness.

"Come on, *galano*," the old man said. "Come in again."

The shark came in a rush and the old man hit him as he shut his jaws. He hit him solidly and from as high up as he could raise the club. This time he felt the bone at the base of the brain and he hit him again in the same place while the shark tore the meat loose sluggishly and slid down from the fish.

The old man watched for him to come again but neither shark showed. Then he saw one on the surface swimming in circles. He did not see the fin of the other.

I could not expect to kill them, he thought. I could have in my time. But I have hurt them both badly and neither one can feel very good. If I could have used a bat with two hands I could have killed the first one surely. Even now, he thought.

He did not want to look at the fish. He knew that half of him had been destroyed. The sun had gone down while he had been in the fight with the sharks.

"I have the gaff now," he said. "But it will do no good. I have the two oars and the tiller and the short club."

Now they have beaten me, he thought. I am too old to club sharks to death. But I will try it as long as I have the oars and the short club and the tiller.

He put his hands in the water again to soak them. It was getting late in the afternoon and he saw nothing but the sea and the sky. There was more wind in the sky than there had been, and soon he hoped that he would see land.

"You're tired, old man," he said. "You're tired inside."

The sharks did not hit him again until just before sunset.

The old man saw the brown fins coming along the wide trail the fish must make in the water. They were not even quartering on the scent. They were headed straight for the skiff swimming side by side.

He jammed the tiller, made the sheet fast and reached under the stern for the club. It was an oar handle from a broken oar sawed off to about two and a half feet in length. He could only use it effectively with one hand because of the grip of the handle and he took good hold of it with his right hand, flexing his hand on it, as he watched the sharks come. They were both *galanos*.

I must let the first one get a good hold and hit him on the point of the nose or straight across the top of the head, he thought.

The two sharks closed together and as he saw the one nearest him open his jaws and sink them into the silver side of the fish, he raised the club high and brought it down heavy and slamming onto the top of the shark's

"You give me much good counsel," he said aloud. "I'm tired of it."

He held the tiller under his arm and soaked both his hands in the water as the skiff drove forward.

"God knows how much that last one took," he said. "But she's much lighter now." He did not want to think of the mutilated under-side of the fish. He knew that each of the jerking bumps of the shark had been meat torn away and that the fish now made a trail for all sharks as wide as a highway through the sea.

He was a fish to keep a man all winter, he thought. Don't think of that. Just rest and try to get your hands in shape to defend what is left of him. The blood smell from my hands means nothing now with all that scent in the water. Besides they do not bleed much. There is nothing cut that means anything. The bleeding may keep the left from cramping.

What can I think of now? he thought. Nothing. I must think of nothing and wait for the next ones. I wish it had really been a dream, he thought. But who knows? It might have turned out well.

The next shark that came was a single shovelnose. He came like a pig to the trough if a pig had a mouth so wide that you could put your head in it. The old man let him hit the fish and then drove the knife on the oar down into his brain. But the shark jerked backwards as he rolled and the knife blade snapped.

The old man settled himself to steer. He did not even watch the big shark sinking slowly in the water, showing first life-size, then small, then tiny. That always fascinated the old man. But he did not even watch it now.

there.

"No?" the old man said and he drove the blade between the vertebrae and the brain. It was an easy shot now and he felt the cartilage sever. The old man reversed the oar and put the blade between the shark's jaws to open them. He twisted the blade and as the shark slid loose he said, "Go on, *galano*. Slide down a mile deep. Go see your friend, or maybe it's your mother."

The old man wiped the blade of his knife and laid down the oar. Then he found the sheet and the sail filled and he brought the skiff onto her course.

"They must have taken a quarter of him and of the best meat," he said aloud. "I wish it were a dream and that I had never hooked him. I'm sorry about it, fish. It makes everything wrong." He stopped and he did not want to look at the fish now. Drained of blood and awash he looked the colour of the silver backing of a minor and his stripes still showed.

"I shouldn't have gone out so far, fish," he said. "Neither for you nor for me. I'm sorry, fish."

Now, he said to himself. Look to the lashing on the knife and see if it has been cut. Then get your hand in order because there still is more to come.

"I wish I had a stone for the knife," the old man said after he had checked the lashing on the oar butt. "I should have brought a stone." You should have brought many things, he thought. But you did not bring them, old man. Now is no time to think of what you do not have. Think of what you can do with what there is.

scavengers as well as killers, and when they were hungry they would bite at an oar or the rudder of a boat. It was these sharks that would cut the turtles' legs and flippers off when the turtles were asleep on the surface, and they would hit a man in the water, if they were hungry, even if the man had no smell of fish blood nor of fish slime on him.

"*Ay*," the old man said. "*Galanos*. Come on *galanos*."

They came. But they did not come as the Mako had come. One turned and went out of sight under the skiff and the old man could feel the skiff shake as he jerked and pulled on the fish. The other watched the old man with his slitted yellow eyes and then came in fast with his half circle of jaws wide to hit the fish where he had already been bitten. The line showed clearly on the top of his brown head and back where the brain joined the spinal cord and the old man drove the knife on the oar into the juncture, withdrew it, and drove it in again into the shark's yellow cat-like eyes. The shark let go of the fish and slid down, swallowing what he had taken as he died.

The skiff was still shaking with the destruction the other shark was doing to the fish and the old man let go the sheet so that the skiff would swing broadside and bring the shark out from under.

When he saw the shark he leaned over the side and punched at him. He hit only meat and the hide was set hard and he barely got the knife in. The blow hurt not only his hands but his shoulder too. But the shark came up fast with his head out and the old man hit him squarely in the center of his flat-topped head as his nose came out of water and lay against the fish. The old man withdrew the blade and punched the shark exactly in the same spot again. He still hung to the fish with his jaws hooked and the old man stabbed him in his left eye. The shark still hung

and the old man knew that a very bad time was coming.

The breeze was steady. It had backed a little further into the north-east and he knew that meant that it would not fall off. The old man looked ahead of him but he could see no sails nor could he see the hull nor the smoke of any ship. There were only the flying fish that went up from his bow sailing away to either side and the yellow patches of Gulf weed. He could not even see a bird.

He had sailed for two hours, resting in the stern and sometimes chewing a bit of the meat from the marlin, trying to rest and to be strong, when he saw the first of the two sharks.

"*Ay,*" he said aloud. There is no translation for this word and perhaps it is just a noise such as a man might make, involuntarily, feeling the nail go through his hands and into the wood.

"*Galanos,*" he said aloud. He had seen the second fin now coming up behind the first and had identified them as shovel-nosed sharks by the brown, triangular fin and the sweeping movements of the tail. They had the scent and were excited and in the stupidity of their great hunger they were losing and finding the scent in their excitement. But they were closing all the time.

The old man made the sheet fast and jammed the tiller. Then he took up the oar with the knife lashed to it. He lifted it as lightly as he could because his hands rebelled at the pain. Then he opened and closed them on it lightly to loosen them. He closed them firmly so they would take the pain now and would not flinch and watched the sharks come. He could see their wide, flattened, shovel-pointed heads now and their white tipped wide pectoral fins. They were hateful sharks, bad smelling,

Perhaps it was a sin to kill the fish. I suppose it was even though I did it to keep me alive and feed many people. But then everything is a sin. Do not think about sin. It is much too late for that and there are people who are paid to do it. Let them think about it. You were born to be a fisherman as the fish was born to be a fish. San Pedro was a fisherman as was the father of the great DiMaggio.

But he liked to think about all things that he was involved in and since there was nothing to read and he did not have a radio, he thought much and he kept on thinking about sin. You did not kill the fish only to keep alive and to sell for food, he thought. You killed him for pride and because you are a fisherman. You loved him when he was alive and you loved him after. If you love him, it is not a sin to kill him. Or is it more?

"You think too much, old man," he said aloud.

But you enjoyed killing the *dentuso,* he thought. He lives on the live fish as you do. He is not a scavenger nor just a moving appetite as some sharks are. He is beautiful and noble and knows no fear of anything.

"I killed him in self-defense," the old man said aloud. "And I killed him well."

Besides, he thought, everything kills everything else in some way. Fishing kills me exactly as it keeps me alive. The boy keeps me alive, he thought. I must not deceive myself too much.

He leaned over the side and pulled loose a piece of the meat of the fish where the shark had cut him. He chewed it and noted its quality and its good taste. It was firm and juicy, like meat, but it was not red. There was no stringiness in it and he knew that it would bring the highest price in the market. But there was no way to keep its scent out of the water

"Don't think, old man," he said aloud. "Sail on this course and take it when it comes."

But I must think, he thought. Because it is all I have left. That and baseball. I wonder how the great DiMaggio would have liked the way I hit him in the brain? It was no great thing, he thought. Any man could do it. But do you think my hands were as great a handicap as the bone spurs? I cannot know. I never had anything wrong with my heel except the time the sting ray stung it when I stepped on him when swimming and paralyzed the lower leg and made the unbearable pain.

"Think about something cheerful, old man," he said. "Every minute now you are closer to home. You sail lighter for the loss of forty pounds."

He knew quite well the pattern of what could happen when he reached the inner part of the current. But there was nothing to be done now.

"Yes there is," he said aloud. "I can lash my knife to the butt of one of the oars."

So he did that with the tiller under his arm and the sheet of the sail under his foot.

"Now," he said. "I am still an old man. But I am not unarmed."

The breeze was fresh now and he sailed on well. He watched only the forward part of the fish and some of his hope returned.

It is silly not to hope, he thought. Besides I believe it is a sin. Do not think about sin, he thought. There are enough problems now without sin. Also I have no understanding of it.

I have no understanding of it and I am not sure that I believe in it.

without hope but with resolution and complete malignancy.

The shark swung over and the old man saw his eye was not alive and then he swung over once again, wrapping himself in two loops of the rope. The old man knew that he was dead but the shark would not accept it. Then, on his back, with his tail lashing and his jaws clicking, the shark plowed over the water as a speedboat does. The water was white where his tail beat it and three-quarters of his body was clear above the water when the rope came taut, shivered, and then snapped. The shark lay quietly for a little while on the surface and the old man watched him. Then he went down very slowly.

"He took about forty pounds," the old man said aloud. He took my harpoon too and all the rope, he thought, and now my fish bleeds again and there will be others.

He did not like to look at the fish anymore since he had been mutilated. When the fish had been hit it was as though he himself were hit.

But I killed the shark that hit my fish, he thought. And he was the biggest *dentuso* that I have ever seen. And God knows that I have seen big ones.

It was too good to last, he thought. I wish it had been a dream now and that I had never hooked the fish and was alone in bed on the newspapers.

"But man is not made for defeat," he said. "A man can be destroyed but not defeated." I am sorry that I killed the fish though, he thought. Now the bad time is coming and I do not even have the harpoon. The *dentuso* is cruel and able and strong and intelligent. But I was more intelligent than he was. Perhaps not, he thought. Perhaps I was only better armed.

of most sharks. They were shaped like a man's fingers when they are crisped like claws. They were nearly as long as the fingers of the old man and they had razor-sharp cutting edges on both sides. This was a fish built to feed on all the fishes in the sea, that were so fast and strong and well armed that they had no other enemy. Now he speeded up as he smelled the fresher scent and his blue dorsal fin cut the water.

When the old man saw him coming he knew that this was a shark that had no fear at all and would do exactly what he wished. He prepared the harpoon and made the rope fast while he watched the shark come on. The rope was short as it lacked what he had cut away to lash the fish.

The old man's head was clear and good now and he was full of resolution but he had little hope. It was too good to last, he thought. He took one look at the great fish as he watched the shark close in. It might as well have been a dream, he thought. I cannot keep him from hitting me but maybe I can get him. *Dentuso,* he thought. Bad luck to your mother.

The shark closed fast astern and when he hit the fish the old man saw his mouth open and his strange eyes and the clicking chop of the teeth as he drove forward in the meat just above the tail. The shark's head was out of water and his back was coming out and the old man could hear the noise of skin and flesh ripping on the big fish when he rammed the harpoon down onto the shark's head at a spot where the line between his eyes intersected with the line that ran straight back from his nose. There were no such lines. There was only the heavy sharp blue head and the big eyes and the clicking, thrusting all-swallowing jaws. But that was the location of the brain and the old man hit it. He hit it with his blood mushed hands driving a good harpoon with all his strength. He hit it little unclear and he thought, is he bringing me in or am I bringing him in? If I were towing him behind there would be no question. Nor if the fish were in the skiff, with all dignity gone, there would be no question either. But they were sailing together lashed side by side and the old man thought, let him bring me in if it pleases him. I am only better than him through trickery and he meant me no harm.

They sailed well and the old man soaked his hands in the salt water and tried to keep his head clear. There were high cumulus clouds and enough cirrus above them so that the old man knew the breeze would last all night. The old man looked at the fish constantly to make sure it was true. It was an hour before the first shark hit him.

The shark was not an accident. He had come up from deep down in the water as the dark cloud of blood had settled and dispersed in the mile deep sea. He had come up so fast and absolutely without caution that he broke the surface of the blue water and was in the sun. Then he fell back into the sea and picked up the scent and started swimming on the course the skiff and the fish had taken.

Sometimes he lost the scent. But he would pick it up again, or have just a trace of it, and he swam fast and hard on the course. He was a very big Mako shark built to swim as fast as the fastest fish in the sea and everything about him was beautiful except his jaws. His back was as blue as a sword fish's and his belly was silver and his hide was smooth and handsome. He was built as a sword fish except for his huge jaws which were tight shut now as he swam fast, just under the surface with his high dorsal fin knifing through the water without wavering. Inside the closed double lip of his jaws all of his eight rows of teeth were slanted inwards. They were not the ordinary pyramid-shaped teeth

He did not need a compass to tell him where southwest was. He only needed the feel of the trade wind and the drawing of the sail. I better put a small line out with a spoon on it and try and get something to eat and drink for the moisture. But he could not find a spoon and his sardines were rotten. So he hooked a patch of yellow Gulf weed with the gaff as they passed and shook it so that the small shrimps that were in it fell onto the planking of the skiff. There were more than a dozen of them and they jumped and kicked like sand fleas. The old man pinched their heads off with his thumb and forefinger and ate them chewing up the shells and the tails. They were very tiny but he knew they were nourishing and they tasted good.

The old man still had two drinks of water in the bottle and he used half of one after he had eaten the shrimps. The skiff was sailing well considering the handicaps and he steered with the tiller under his arm. He could see the fish and he had only to look at his hands and feel his back against the stern to know that this had truly happened and was not a dream. At one time when he was feeling so badly toward the end, he had thought perhaps it was a dream. Then when he had seen the fish come out of the water and hang motionless in the sky before he fell, he was sure there was some great strangeness and he could not believe it. Then he could not see well, although now he saw as well as ever.

Now he knew there was the fish and his hands and back were no dream. The hands cure quickly, he thought. I bled them clean and the salt water will heal them. The dark water of the true gulf is the greatest healer that there is. All I must do is keep the head clear. The hands have done their work and we sail well. With his mouth shut and his tail straight up and down we sail like brothers. Then his head started to become a wallowing now in the seas and the old man pulled the skiff up-onto him.

When he was even with him and had the fish's head against the bow he could not believe his size. But he untied the harpoon rope from the bitt, passed it through the fish's gills and out his jaws, made a turn around his sword then passed the rope through the other gill, made another turn around the bill and knotted the double rope and made it fast to the bitt in the bow. He cut the rope then and went astern to noose the tail. The fish had turned silver from his original purple and silver, and the stripes showed the same pale violet colour as his tail. They were wider than a man's hand with his fingers spread and the fish's eye looked as detached as the mirrors in a periscope or as a saint in a procession.

"It was the only way to kill him," the old man said. He was feeling better since the water and he knew he would not go away and his head was clear. He's over fifteen hundred pounds the way he is, he thought. Maybe much more. If he dresses out two-thirds of that at thirty cents a pound?

"I need a pencil for that," he said. "My head is not that clear. But I think the great DiMaggio would be proud of me today. I had no bone spurs. But the hands and the back hurt truly." I wonder what a bone spur is, he thought. Maybe we have them without knowing of it.

He made the fish fast to bow and stern and to the middle thwart. He was so big it was like lashing a much bigger skiff alongside. He cut a piece of line and tied the fish's lower jaw against his bill so his mouth would not open and they would sail as cleanly as possible. Then he stepped the mast and, with the stick that was his gaff and with his boom rigged, the patched sail drew, the boat began to move, and half lying in the stern he sailed south-west.

The old man looked carefully in the glimpse of vision that he had. Then he took two turns of the harpoon line around the bitt in the bow and laid his head on his hands.

"Keep my head dear," he said against the wood of the bow. "I am a tired old man. But I have killed this fish which is my brother and now I must do the slave work."

Now I must prepare the nooses and the rope to lash him alongside, he thought. Even if we were two and swamped her to load him and bailed her out, this skiff would never hold him. I must prepare everything, then bring him in and lash him well and step the mast and set sail for home.

He started to pull the fish in to have him alongside so that he could pass a line through his gills and out his mouth and make his head fast alongside the bow. I want to see him, he thought, and to touch and to feel him. He is my fortune, he thought. But that is not why I wish to feel him. I think I felt his heart, he thought. When I pushed on the harpoon shaft the second time. Bring him in now and make him fast and get the noose around his tail and another around his middle to bind him to the skiff.

"Get to work, old man," he said. He took a very small drink of the water. "There is very much slave work to be done now that the fight is over."

He looked up at the sky and then out to his fish. He looked at the sun carefully. It is not much more than noon, he thought. And the trade wind is rising. The lines all mean nothing now. The boy and I will splice them when we are home.

"Come on, fish," he said. But the fish did not come. Instead he lay there

He tried it again and it was the same. So he thought, and he felt himself going before he started; I will try it once again.

He took all his pain and what was left of his strength and his long gone pride and he put it against the fish's agony and the fish came over onto his side and swam gently on his side, his bill almost touching the planking of the skiff and started to pass the boat, long, deep, wide, silver and barred with purple and interminable in the water.

The old man dropped the line and put his foot on it and lifted the harpoon as high as he could and drove it down with all his strength, and more strength he had just summoned, into the fish's side just behind the great chest fin that rose high in the air to the altitude of the man's chest. He felt the iron go in and he leaned on it and drove it further and then pushed all his weight after it.

Then the fish came alive, with his death in him, and rose high out of the water showing all his great length and width and all his power and his beauty. He seemed to hang in the air above the old man in the skiff. Then he fell into the water with a crash that sent spray over the old man and over all of the skiff.

The old man felt faint and sick and he could not see well. But he cleared the harpoon line and let it run slowly through his raw hands and, when he could see, he saw the fish was on his back with his silver belly up. The shaft of the harpoon was projecting at an angle from the fish's shoulder and the sea was discolouring with the red of the blood from his heart. First it was dark as a shoal in the blue water that was more than a mile deep. Then it spread like a cloud. The fish was silvery and still and floated with the waves.

"Fish," the old man said. "Fish, you are going to have to die anyway. Do you have to kill me too?"

That way nothing is accomplished, he thought. His mouth was too dry to speak but he could not reach for the water now. I must get him alongside this time, he thought. I am not good for many more turns. Yes you are, he told himself. You're good for ever.

On the next turn, he nearly had him. But again the fish righted himself and swam slowly away.

You are killing me, fish, the old man thought. But you have a right to. Never have I seen a greater, or more beautiful, or a calmer or more noble thing than you, brother. Come on and kill me. I do not care who kills who.

Now you are getting confused in the head, he thought. You must keep your head clear. Keep your head clear and know how to suffer like a man. Or a fish, he thought.

"Clear up, head," he said in a voice he could hardly hear. "Clear up." Twice more it was the same on the turns.

I do not know, the old man thought. He had been on the point of feeling himself go each time. I do not know. But I will try it once more.

He tried it once more and he felt himself going when he turned the fish. The fish righted himself and swam off again slowly with the great tail weaving in the air.

I'll try it again, the old man promised, although his hands were mushy now and he could only see well in flashes.

The old man was sweating now but from something else besides the sun. On each calm placid turn the fish made he was gaining line and he was sure that in two turns more he would have a chance to get the harpoon in.

But I must get him close, close, close, he thought. I mustn't try for the head. I must get the heart.

"Be calm and strong, old man," he said.

On the next circle the fish's beck was out but he was a little too far from the boat. On the next circle he was still too far away but he was higher out of water and the old man was sure that by gaining some more line he could have him alongside.

He had rigged his harpoon long before and its coil of light rope was in a round basket and the end was made fast to the bitt in the bow.

The fish was coming in on his circle now calm and beautiful looking and only his great tail moving. The old man pulled on him all that he could to bring him closer. For just a moment the fish turned a little on his side. Then he straightened himself and began another circle.

"I moved him," the old man said. "I moved him then."

He felt faint again now but he held on the great fish all the strain that he could. I moved him, he thought. Maybe this time I can get him over. Pull, hands, he thought. Hold up, legs. Last for me, head. Last for me. You never went. This time I'll pull him over.

But when he put all of his effort on, starting it well out before the fish came alongside and pulling with all his strength, the fish pulled part way over and then righted himself and swam away.

"I'll rest on the next turn as he goes out," he said. "I feel much better. Then in two or three turns more I will have him."

His straw hat was far on the back of his head and he sank down into the bow with the pull of the line as he felt the fish turn.

You work now, fish, he thought. I'll take you at the turn.

The sea had risen considerably. But it was a fair-weather breeze and he had to have it to get home.

"I'll just steer south and west," he said. "A man is never lost at sea and it is a long island."

It was on the third turn that he saw the fish first.

He saw him first as a dark shadow that took so long to pass under the boat that he could not believe its length.

"No," he said. "He can't be that big."

But he was that big and at the end of this circle he came to the surface only thirty yards away and the man saw his tail out of water. It was higher than a big scythe blade and a very pale lavender above the dark blue water. It raked back and as the fish swam just below the surface the old man could see his huge bulk and the purple stripes that banded him. His dorsal fin was down and his huge pectorals were spread wide.

On this circle the old man could see the fish's eye and the two gray sucking fish that swain around him. Sometimes they attached themselves to him. Sometimes they darted off. Sometimes they would swim easily in his shadow. They were each over three feet long and when they swam fast they lashed their whole bodies like eels.

rather he stayed circling now. The jumps were necessary for him to take air. But after that each one can widen the opening of the hook wound and he can throw the hook.

"Don't jump, fish," he said. "Don't jump."

The fish hit the wire several times more and each time he shook his head the old man gave up a little line.

I must hold his pain where it is, he thought. Mine does not matter. I can control mine. But his pain could drive him mad.

After a while the fish stopped beating at the wire and started circling slowly again. The old man was gaining line steadily now. But he felt faint again. He lifted some sea water with his left hand and put it on his head. Then he put more on and rubbed the back of his neck.

"I have no cramps," he said. "He'll be up soon and I can last. You have to last. Don't even speak of it."

He kneeled against the bow and, for a moment, slipped the line over his back again. I'll rest now while he goes out on the circle and then stand up and work on him when he comes in, he decided.

It was a great temptation to rest in the bow and let the fish make one circle by himself without recovering any line. But when the strain showed the fish had turned to come toward the boat, the old man rose to his feet and started the pivoting and the weaving pulling that brought in all the line he gained.

I'm tireder than I have ever been, he thought, and now the trade wind is rising. But that will be good to take him in with. I need that badly.

"It is a very big circle," he said. "But he is circling."

Then the line would not come in any more and he held it until he saw the drops jumping from it in the sun. Then it started out and the old man knelt down and let it go grudgingly back into the dark water.

"He is making the far part of his circle now," he said. I must hold all I can, he thought. The strain will shorten his circle each time. Perhaps in an hour I will see him. Now I must convince him and then I must kill him.

But the fish kept on circling slowly and the old man was wet with sweat and tired deep into his bones two hours later. But the circles were much shorter now and from the way the line slanted he could tell the fish had risen steadily while he swam.

For an hour the old man had been seeing black spots before his eyes and the sweat salted his eyes and salted the cut over his eye and on his forehead. He was not afraid of the black spots. They were normal at the tension that he was pulling on the line. Twice, though, he had felt faint and dizzy and that had worried him.

"I could not fail myself and die on a fish like this," he said. "Now that I have him coming so beautifully, God help me endure. I'll say a hundred Our Fathers and a hundred Hail Marys. But I cannot say them now."

Consider them said, he thought. I'll say them later.

Just then he felt a sudden banging and jerking on the line he held with his two hands. It was sharp and hard-feeling and heavy.

He is hitting the wire leader with his spear, he thought. That was bound to come. He had to do that. It may make him jump though and I would and he has only cramped once. If he cramps again let the line cut him off.

When he thought that he knew that he was not being clear-headed and he thought he should chew some more of the dolphin. But I can't, he told himself. It is better to be light-headed than to lose your strength from nausea. And I know I cannot keep it if I eat it since my face was in it. I will keep it for an emergency until it goes bad. But it is too late to try for strength now through nourishment. You're stupid, he told himself. Eat the other flying fish.

It was there, cleaned and ready, and he picked it up with his left hand and ate it chewing the bones carefully and eating all of it down to the tail.

It has more nourishment than almost any fish, he thought. At least the kind of strength that I need. Now I have done what I can, he thought. Let him begin to circle and let the fight come.

The sun was rising for the third time since he had put to sea when the fish started to circle.

He could not see by the slant of the line that the fish was circling. It was too early for that. He just felt a faint slackening of the pressure of the line and he commenced to pull on it gently with his right hand. It tightened, as always, but just when he reached the point where it would break, line began to come in. He slipped his shoulders and head from under the line and began to pull in line steadily and gently. He used both of his hands in a swinging motion and tried to do the pulling as much as he could with his body and his legs. His old legs and shoulders pivoted with the swinging of the pulling.

it have been hunger that made him desperate, or was he frightened by something in the night? Maybe he suddenly felt fear. But he was such a calm, strong fish and he seemed so fearless and so confident. It is strange.

"You better be fearless and confident yourself, old man," he said. "You're holding him again but you cannot get line. But soon he has to circle."

The old man held him with his left hand and his shoulders now and stooped down and scooped up water in his right hand to get the crushed dolphin flesh off of his face. He was afraid that it might nauseate him and he would vomit and lose his strength. When his face was cleaned he washed his right hand in the water over the side and then let it stay in the salt water while he watched the first light come before the sunrise. He's headed almost east, he thought. That means he is tired and going with the current. Soon he will have to circle. Then our true work begins.

After he judged that his right hand had been in the water long enough he took it out and looked at it.

"It is not bad," he said. "And pain does not matter to a man."

He took hold of the line carefully so that it did not fit into any of the fresh line cuts and shifted his weight so that he could put his left hand into the sea on the other side of the skiff.

"You did not do so badly for something worthless," he said to his left hand. "But there was a moment when I could not find you."

Why was I not born with two good hands? he thought. Perhaps it was my fault in not training that one properly. But God knows he has had enough chances to learn. He did not do so badly in the night, though, great bursting of the ocean and then a heavy fall. Then he jumped again and again and the boat was going fast although line was still racing out and the old man was raising the strain to breaking point and raising it to breaking point again and again. He had been pulled down tight onto the bow and his face was in the cut slice of dolphin and he could not move.

This is what we waited for, he thought. So now let us take it.

Make him pay for the line, he thought. Make him pay for it.

He could not see the fish's jumps but only heard the breaking of the ocean and the heavy splash as he fell. The speed of the line was cutting his hands badly but he had always known this would happen and he tried to keep the cutting across the calloused parts and not let the line slip into the palm nor cut the fingers.

If the boy was here he would wet the coils of line, he thought. Yes. If the boy were here. If the boy were here.

The line went out and out and out but it was slowing now and he was making the fish earn each inch of it. Now he got his head up from the wood and out of the slice of fish that his cheek had crushed. Then he was on his knees and then he rose slowly to his feet. He was ceding line but more slowly all the time. He worked back to where he could feel with his foot the coils of line that he could not see. There was plenty of line still and now the fish had to pull the friction of all that new line through the water.

Yes, he thought. And now he has jumped more than a dozen times and filled the sacks along his back with air and he cannot go down deep to die where I cannot bring him up. He will start circling soon and then I must work on him. I wonder what started him so suddenly? Could

in sleep my left hand will wake me as the line goes out. It is hard on the right hand. But he is used to punishment. Even if I sleep twenty minutes or a half an hour it is good. He lay forward cramping himself against the line with all of his body, putting all his weight onto his right hand, and he was asleep.

He did not dream of the lions but instead of a vast school of porpoises that stretched for eight or ten miles and it was in the time of their mating and they would leap high into the air and return into the same hole they had made in the water when they leaped.

Then he dreamed that he was in the village on his bed and there was a norther and he was very cold and his right arm was asleep because his head had rested on it instead of a pillow.

After that he began to dream of the long yellow beach and he saw the first of the lions come down onto it in the early dark and then the other lions came and he rested his chin on the wood of the bows where the ship lay anchored with the evening off-shore breeze and he waited to see if there would be more lions and he was happy.

The moon had been up for a long time but he slept on and the fish pulled on steadily and the boat moved into the tunnel of clouds.

He woke with the jerk of his right fist coming up against his face and the line burning out through his right hand. He had no feeling of his left hand but he braked all he could with his right and the line rushed out. Finally his left hand found the line and he leaned back against the line and now it burned his back and his left hand, and his left hand was taking all the strain and cutting badly. He looked back at the coils of line and they were feeding smoothly. Just then the fish jumped making a water against it. The flow was less strong and as he rubbed the side of his hand against the planking of the skiff, particles of phosphorus floated off and drifted slowly astern.

"He is tiring or he is resting," the old man said. "Now let me get through the eating of this dolphin and get some rest and a little sleep."

Under the stars and with the night colder all the time he ate half of one of the dolphin fillets and one of the flying fish, gutted and with its head cut off.

"What an excellent fish dolphin is to eat cooked," he said. "And what a miserable fish raw. I will never go in a boat again without salt or limes."

If I had brains I would have splashed water on the bow all day and drying, it would have made salt, he thought. But then I did not hook the dolphin until almost sunset. Still it was a lack of preparation. But I have chewed it all well and I am not nauseated.

The sky was clouding over to the east and one after another the stars he knew were gone. It looked now as though he were moving into a great canyon of clouds and the wind had dropped.

"There will be bad weather in three or four days," he said. "But not tonight and not tomorrow. Rig now to get some sleep, old man, while the fish is calm and steady."

He held the line tight in his right hand and then pushed his thigh against his right hand as he leaned all his weight against the wood of the bow. Then he passed the line a little lower on his shoulders and braced his left hand on it.

My right hand can hold it as long as it is braced, he thought. If it relaxes

Back in the stern he turned so that his left hand held the strain of the line across his shoulders and drew his knife from its sheath with his right hand. The stars were bright now and he saw the dolphin clearly and he pushed the blade of his knife into his head and drew him out from under the stern. He put one of his feet on the fish and slit him quickly from the vent up to the tip of his lower jaw. Then he put his knife down and gutted him with his right hand, scooping him clean and pulling the gills clear. He felt the maw heavy and slippery in his hands and he slit it open. There were two flying fish inside. They were fresh and hard and he laid them side by side and dropped the guts and the gills over the stern. They sank leaving a trail of phosphorescence in the water. The dolphin was cold and a leprous gray-white now in the starlight and the old man skinned one side of him while he held his right foot on the fish's head. Then he turned him over and skinned the other side and cut each side off from the head down to the tail.

He slid the carcass overboard and looked to see if there was any swirl in the water. But there was only the light of its slow descent. He turned then and placed the two flying fish inside the two fillets of fish and putting his knife back in its sheath, he worked his way slowly back to the bow. His back was bent with the weight of the line across it and he carried the fish in his right hand.

Back in the bow he laid the two fillets of fish out on the wood with the flying fish beside them. After that he settled the line across his shoulders in a new place and held it again with his left hand resting on the gunwale. Then he leaned over the side and washed the flying fish in the water, noting the speed of the water against his hand. His hand was phosphorescent from skinning the fish and he watched the flow of the

He rested for what he believed to be two hours. The moon did not rise now until late and he had no way of judging the time. Nor was he really resting except comparatively. He was still bearing the pull of the fish across his shoulders but he placed his left hand on the gunwale of the bow and confided more and more of the resistance to the fish to the skiff itself.

How simple it would be if I could make the line fast, he thought. But with one small lurch he could break it. I must cushion the pull of the line with my body and at all times be ready to give line with both hands.

"But you have not slept yet, old man," he said aloud. "It is half a day and a night and now another day and you have not slept. You must devise a way so that you sleep a little if he is quiet and steady. If you do not sleep you might become unclear in the head."

I'm clear enough in the head, he thought. Too clear. I am as clear as the stars that are my brothers. Still I must sleep. They sleep and the moon and the sun sleep and even the ocean sleeps sometimes on certain days when there is no current and a flat calm.

But remember to sleep, he thought. Make yourself do it and devise some simple and sure way about the lines. Now go back and prepare the dolphin. It is too dangerous to rig the oars as a drag if you must sleep.

I could go without sleeping, he told himself. But it would be too dangerous.

He started to work his way back to the stern on his hands and knees, being careful not to jerk against the fish. He may be half asleep himself, he thought. But I do not want him to rest. He must pull until he dies.

Imagine if each day a man must try to kill the moon, he thought. The moon runs away. But imagine if a man each day should have to try to kill the sun? We were born lucky, he thought.

Then he was sorry for the great fish that had nothing to eat and his determination to kill him never relaxed in his sorrow for him. How many people will he feed, he thought. But are they worthy to eat him? No, of course not. There is no one worthy of eating him from the manner of his behaviour and his great dignity.

I do not understand these things, he thought. But it is good that we do not have to try to kill the sun or the moon or the stars. It is enough to live on the sea and kill our true brothers.

Now, he thought, I must think about the drag. It has its perils and its merits. I may lose so much line that I will lose him, if he makes his effort and the drag made by the oars is in place and the boat loses all her lightness. Her lightness prolongs both our suffering but it is my safety since he has great speed that he has never yet employed. No matter what passes I must gut the dolphin so he does not spoil and eat some of him to be strong.

Now I will rest an hour more and feel that he is solid and steady before I move back to the stern to do the work and make the decision. In the meantime I can see how he acts and if he shows any changes. The oars are a good trick; but it has reached the time to play for safety. He is much fish still and I saw that the hook was in the corner of his mouth and he has kept his mouth tight shut. The punishment of the hook is nothing. The punishment of hunger, and that he is against something that he does not comprehend, is everything. Rest now, old man, and let him work until your next duty comes.

for all fish.

He let his hand dry in the air then grasped the line with it and eased himself as much as he could and allowed himself to be pulled forward against the wood so that the boat took the strain as much, or more, than he did.

I'm learning how to do it, he thought. This part of it anyway. Then too, remember he hasn't eaten since he took the bait and he is huge and needs much food. I have eaten the whole bonito. Tomorrow I will eat the dolphin. He called it *dorado*. Perhaps I should eat some of it when I clean it. It will be harder to eat than the bonito. But, then, nothing is easy.

"How do you feel, fish?" he asked aloud. "I feel good and my left hand is better and I have food for a night and a day. Pull the boat, fish."

He did not truly feel good because the pain from the cord across his back had almost passed pain and gone into a dullness that he mistrusted. But I have had worse things than that, he thought. My hand is only cut a little and the cramp is gone from the other. My legs are all right. Also now I have gained on him in the question of sustenance.

It was dark now as it becomes dark quickly after the sun sets in September. He lay against the worn wood of the bow and rested all that he could. The first stars were out. He did not know the name of Rigel but he saw it and knew soon they would all be out and he would have all his distant friends.

"The fish is my friend too," he said aloud. "I have never seen or heard of such a fish. But I must kill him. I am glad we do not have to try to kill the stars."

love with something under a yellow blanket, his small line was taken by a dolphin. He saw it first when it jumped in the air, true gold in the last of the sun and bending and flapping wildly in the air. It jumped again and again in the acrobatics of its fear and he worked his way back to the stern and crouching and holding the big line with his right hand and arm, he pulled the dolphin in with his left hand, stepping on the gained line each time with his bare left foot. When the fish was at the stern, plunging and cutting from side to side in desperation, the old man leaned over the stern and lifted the burnished gold fish with its purple spots over the stem. Its jaws were working convulsively in quick bites against the hook and it pounded the bottom of the skiff with its long flat body, its tail and its head until he clubbed it across the shining golden head until it shivered and was still.

The old man unhooked the fish, re-baited the line with another sardine and tossed it over. Then he worked his way slowly back to the bow. He washed his left hand and wiped it on his trousers. Then he shifted the heavy line from his right hand to his left and washed his right hand in the sea while he watched the sun go into the ocean and the slant of the big cord.

"He hasn't changed at all," he said. But watching the movement of the water against his hand he noted that it was perceptibly slower.

"I'll lash the two oars together across the stern and that will slow him in the night," he said. "He's good for the night and so am I."

It would be better to gut the dolphin a little later to save the blood in the meat, he thought. I can do that a little later and lash the oars to make a drag at the same time. I had better keep the fish quiet now and not disturb him too much at sunset. The setting of the sun is a difficult time his left hand had always been a traitor and would not do what he called on it to do and he did not trust it.

The sun will bake it out well now, he thought. It should not cramp on me again unless it gets too cold in the night. I wonder what this night will bring.

An airplane passed overhead on its course to Miami and he watched its shadow scaring up the schools of flying fish.

"With so much flying fish there should be dolphin," he said, and leaned back on the line to see if it was possible to gain any on his fish. But he could not and it stayed at the hardness and water-drop shivering that preceded breaking. The boat moved ahead slowly and he watched the airplane until he could no longer see it.

It must be very strange in an airplane, he thought. I wonder what the sea looks like from that height? They should be able to see the fish well if they do not fly too high. I would like to fly very slowly at two hundred fathoms high and see the fish from above. In the turtle boats I was in the cross-trees of the mast-head and even at that height I saw much. The dolphin look greener from there and you can see their stripes and their purple spots and you can see all of the school as they swim. Why is it that all the fast-moving fish of the dark current have purple backs and usually purple stripes or spots? The dolphin looks green of course because he is really golden. But when he comes to feed, truly hungry, purple stripes show on his sides as on a marlin. Can it be anger, or the greater speed he makes that brings them out?

Just before it was dark, as they passed a great island of Sargasso weed that heaved and swung in the light sea as though the ocean were making

each other in the eye and at their hands and forearms and the bettors went in and out of the room and sat on high chairs against the wall and watched. The walls were painted bright blue and were of wood and the lamps threw their shadows against them. The negro's shadow was huge and it moved on the wall as the breeze moved the lamps.

The odds would change back and forth all night and they fed the negro rum and lighted cigarettes for him. Then the negro, after the rum, would try for a tremendous effort and once he had the old man, who was not an old man then but was Santiago *El Campeón,* nearly three inches off balance. But the old man had raised his hand up to dead even again. He was sure then that he had the negro, who was a fine man and a great athlete, beaten. And at daylight when the bettors were asking that it be called a draw and the referee was shaking his head, he had unleashed his effort and forced the hand of the negro down and down until it rested on the wood. The match had started on a Sunday morning and ended on a Monday morning. Many of the bettors had asked for a draw because they had to go to work on the docks loading sacks of sugar or at the Havana Coal Company. Otherwise everyone would have wanted it to go to a finish. But he had finished it anyway and before anyone had to go to work.

For a long time after that everyone had called him The Champion and there had been a return match in the spring. But not much money was bet and he had won it quite easily since he had broken the confidence of the negro from Cienfuegos in the first match. After that he had a few matches and then no more. He decided that he could beat anyone if he wanted to badly enough and he decided that it was bad for his right hand for fishing. He had tried a few practice matches with his left hand. But

This is the second day now that I do not know the result of the *juegos,* he thought. But I must have confidence and I must be worthy of the great DiMaggio who does all things perfectly even with the pain of the bone spur in his heel. What is a bone spur? he asked himself. *Un espuela de hueso.* We do not have them. Can it be as painful as the spur of a fighting cock in one's heel? I do not think I could endure that or the loss of the eye and of both eyes and continue to fight as the fighting cocks do. Man is not much beside the great birds and beasts. Still I would rather be that beast down there in the darkness of the sea.

"Unless sharks come," he said aloud. "If sharks come, God pity him and me."

Do you believe the great DiMaggio would stay with a fish as long as I will stay with this one? he thought. I am sure he would and more since he is young and strong. Also his father was a fisherman. But would the bone spur hurt him too much?

"I do not know," he said aloud. "I never had a bone spur."

As the sun set he remembered, to give himself more confidence, the time in the tavern at Casablanca when he had played the hand game with the great negro from Cienfuegos who was the strongest man on the docks. They had gone one day and one night with their elbows on a chalk line on the table and their forearms straight up and their hands gripped tight. Each one was trying to force the other's hand down onto the table. There was much betting and people went in and out of the room under the kerosene lights and he had looked at the arm and hand of the negro and at the negro's face. They changed the referees every four hours after the first eight so that the referees could sleep. Blood came out from under the fingernails of both his and the negro's hands and they looked

thought. Why are the lions the main thing that is left? Don't think, old man, he said to himself, Rest gently now against the wood and think of nothing. He is working. Work as little as you can.

It was getting into the afternoon and the boat still moved slowly and steadily. But there was an added drag now from the easterly breeze and the old man rode gently with the small sea and the hurt of the cord across his back came to him easily and smoothly.

Once in the afternoon the line started to rise again. But the fish only continued to swim at a slightly higher level. The sun was on the old man's left arm and shoulder and on his back. So he knew the fish had turned east of north.

Now that he had seen him once, he could picture the fish swimming in the water with his purple pectoral fins set wide as wings and the great erect tail slicing through the dark. I wonder how much he sees at that depth, the old man thought. His eye is huge and a horse, with much less eye, can see in the dark. Once I could see quite well in the dark. Not in the absolute dark. But almost as a cat sees.

The sun and his steady movement of his fingers had uncramped his left hand now completely and he began to shift more of the strain to it and he shrugged the muscles of his back to shift the hurt of the cord a little.

"If you're not tired, fish," he said aloud, "you must be very strange."

He felt very tired now and he knew the night would come soon and he tried to think of other things. He thought of the Big Leagues, to him they were the *Gran Ligas,* and he knew that the Yankees of New York were playing the *Tigres* of Detroit.

"Hail Mary full of Grace the Lord is with thee. Blessed art thou among women and blessed is the fruit of thy womb, Jesus. Holy Mary, Mother of God, pray for us sinners now and at the hour of our death. Amen." Then he added, "Blessed Virgin, pray for the death of this fish. Wonderful though he is."

With his prayers said, and feeling much better, but suffering exactly as much, and perhaps a little more, he leaned against the wood of the bow and began, mechanically, to work the fingers of his left hand.

The sun was hot now although the breeze was rising gently.

"I had better re-bait that little line out over the stern," he said. "If the fish decides to stay another night I will need to eat again and the water is low in the bottle. I don't think I can get anything but a dolphin here. But if I eat him fresh enough he won't be bad. I wish a flying fish would come on board tonight. But I have no light to attract them. A flying fish is excellent to eat raw and I would not have to cut him up. I must save all my strength now. Christ, I did not know he was so big."

"I'll kill him though," he said. "In all his greatness and his glory."

Although it is unjust, he thought. But I will show him what a man can do and what a man endures.

"I told the boy I was a strange old man," he said. "Now is when I must prove it."

The thousand times that he had proved it meant nothing. Now he was proving it again. Each time was a new time and he never thought about the past when he was doing it.

I wish he'd sleep and I could sleep and dream about the lions, he

It will uncramp though, he thought. Surely it will uncramp to help my right hand. There are three things that are brothers: the fish and my two hands. It must uncramp. It is unworthy of it to be cramped. The fish had slowed again and was going at his usual pace.

I wonder why he jumped, the old man thought. He jumped almost as though to show me how big he was. I know now, anyway, he thought. I wish I could show him what sort of man I am. But then he would see the cramped hand. Let him think I am more man than I am and I will be so. I wish I was the fish, he thought, with everything he has against only my will and my intelligence.

He settled comfortably against the wood and took his suffering as it came and the fish swam steadily and the boat moved slowly through the dark water. There was a small sea rising with the wind coming up from the east and at noon the old man's left hand was uncramped.

"Bad news for you, fish," he said and shifted the line over the sacks that covered his shoulders.

He was comfortable but suffering, although he did not admit the suffering at all.

"I am not religious," he said. "But I will say ten Our Fathers and ten Hail Marys that I should catch this fish, and I promise to make a pilgrimage to the Virgin of Cobre if I catch him. That is a promise."

He commenced to say his prayers mechanically. Sometimes he would be so tired that he could not remember the prayer and then he would say them fast so that they would come automatically. Hail Marys are easier to say than Our Fathers, he thought.

the line and slapped his left hand hard and fast against his thigh he saw the line slanting slowly upward.

"He's coming up," he said. "Come on hand. Please come on."

The line rose slowly and steadily and then the surface of the ocean bulged ahead of the boat and the fish came out. He came out unendingly and water poured from his sides. He was bright in the sun and his head and back were dark purple and in the sun the stripes on his sides showed wide and a light lavender. His sword was as long as a baseball bat and tapered like a rapier and he rose his full length from the water and then re-entered it, smoothly, like a diver and the old man saw the great scythe- blade of his tail go under and the line commenced to race out.

"He is two feet longer than the skiff," the old man said. The line was going out fast but steadily and the fish was not panicked. The old man was trying with both hands to keep the line just inside of breaking strength. He knew that if he could not slow the fish with a steady pressure the fish could take out all the line and break it.

He is a great fish and I must convince him, he thought. I must never let him learn his strength nor what he could do if he made his run. If I were him I would put in everything now and go until something broke. But, thank God, they are not as intelligent as we who kill them; although they are more noble and more able.

The old man had seen many great fish. He had seen many that weighed more than a thousand pounds and he had caught two of that size in his life, but never alone. Now alone, and out of sight of land, he was fast to the biggest fish that he had ever seen and bigger than he had ever heard of, and his left hand was still as tight as the gripped claws of an eagle.

the strange undulation of the calm. The clouds were building up now for the trade wind and he looked ahead and saw a flight of wild ducks etching themselves against the sky over the water, then blurring, then etching again and he knew no man was ever alone on the sea.

He thought of how some men feared being out of sight of land in a small boat and knew they were right in the months of sudden bad weather. But now they were in hurricane months and, when there are no hurricanes, the weather of hurricane months is the best of all the year.

If there is a hurricane you always see the signs of it in the sky for days ahead, if you are at sea. They do not see it ashore because they do not know what to look for, he thought. The land must make a difference too, in the shape of the clouds. But we have no hurricane coming now.

He looked at the sky and saw the white cumulus built like friendly piles of ice cream and high above were the thin feathers of the cirrus against the high September sky.

"Light *brisa*," he said. "Better weather for me than for you, fish."

His left hand was still cramped, but he was unknotting it slowly.

I hate a cramp, he thought. It is a treachery of one's own body. It is humiliating before others to have a diarrhoea from ptomaine poisoning or to vomit from it. But a cramp, he thought of it as a *calambre*, humiliates oneself especially when one is alone.

If the boy were here he could rub it for me and loosen it down from the forearm, he thought. But it will loosen up.

Then, with his right hand he felt the difference in the pull of the line before he saw the slant change in the water. Then, as he leaned against is calm and steady. I will eat it all and then I will be ready.

"Be patient, hand," he said. "I do this for you."

I wish I could feed the fish, he thought. He is my brother. But I must kill him and keep strong to do it. Slowly and conscientiously he ate all of the wedge-shaped strips of fish.

He straightened up, wiping his hand on his trousers.

"Now," he said. "You can let the cord go, hand, and I will handle him with the right arm alone until you stop that nonsense." He put his left foot on the heavy line that the left hand had held and lay back against the pull against his back.

"God help me to have the cramp go," he said. "Because I do not know what the fish is going to do."

But he seems calm, he thought, and following his plan. But what is his plan, he thought. And what is mine? Mine I must improvise to his because of his great size. If he will jump I can kill him. But he stays down forever. Then I will stay down with him forever.

He rubbed the cramped hand against his trousers and tried to gentle the fingers. But it would not open. Maybe it will open with the sun, he thought. Maybe it will open when the strong raw tuna is digested. If I have to have it, I will open it, cost whatever it costs. But I do not want to open it now by force. Let it open by itself and come back of its own accord. After all I abused it much in the night when it was necessary to free and untie the various lines.

He looked across the sea and knew how alone he was now. But he could see the prisms in the deep dark water and the line stretching ahead and

left hand was cramped. It drew up tight on the heavy cord and he looked at it in disgust.

"What kind of a hand is that," he said. "Cramp then if you want. Make yourself into a claw. It will do you no good."

Come on, he thought and looked down into the dark water at the slant of the line. Eat it now and it will strengthen the hand. It is not the hand's fault and you have been many hours with the fish. But you can stay with him forever. Eat the bonito now.

He picked up a piece and put it in his mouth and chewed it slowly. It was not unpleasant.

Chew it well, he thought, and get all the juices. It would not be bad to eat with a little lime or with lemon or with salt.

"How do you feel, hand?" he asked the cramped hand that was almost as stiff as rigor mortis. "I'll eat some more for you."

He ate the other part of the piece that he had cut in two. He chewed it carefully and then spat out the skin.

"How does it go, hand? Or is it too early to know?"

He took another full piece and chewed it.

"It is a strong full-blooded fish," he thought. "I was lucky to get him instead of dolphin. Dolphin is too sweet. This is hardly sweet at all and all the strength is still in it."

There is no sense in being anything but practical though, he thought. I wish I had some salt. And I do not know whether the sun will rot or dry what is left, so I had better eat it all although I am not hungry. The fish

"I wish the boy were here and that I had some salt," he said aloud. Shifting the weight of the line to his left shoulder and kneeling carefully he washed his hand in the ocean and held it there, submerged, for more than a minute watching the blood trail away and the steady movement of the water against his hand as the boat moved.

"He has slowed much," he said.

The old man would have liked to keep his hand in the salt water longer but he was afraid of another sudden lurch by the fish and he stood up and braced himself and held his hand up against the sun. It was only a line burn that had cut his flesh. But it was in the working part of his hand. He knew he would need his hands before this was over and he did not like to be cut before it started.

"Now," he said, when his hand had dried, "I must eat the small tuna. I can reach him with the gaff and eat him here in comfort."

He knelt down and found the tuna under the stern with the gaff and drew it toward him keeping it clear of the coiled lines. Holding the line with his left shoulder again, and bracing on his left hand and arm, he took the tuna off the gaff hook and put the gaff back in place. He put one knee on the fish and cut strips of dark red meat longitudinally from the back of the head to the tail. They were wedge-shaped strips and he cut them from next to the back bone down to the edge of the belly. When he had cut six strips he spread them out on the wood of the bow, wiped his knife on his trousers, and lifted the carcass of the bonito by the tail and dropped it overboard.

"I don't think I can eat an entire one," he said and drew his knife across one of the strips. He could feel the steady hard pull of the line and his

"Take a good rest, small bird," he said. "Then go in and take your chance like any man or bird or fish."

It encouraged him to talk because his back had stiffened in the night and it hurt truly now.

"Stay at my house if you like, bird," he said. "I am sorry I cannot hoist the sail and take you in with the small breeze that is rising. But I am with a friend."

Just then the fish gave a sudden lurch that pulled the old man down onto the bow and would have pulled him overboard if he had not braced himself and given some line.

The bird had flown up when the line jerked and the old man had not even seen him go. He felt the line carefully with his right hand and noticed his hand was bleeding.

"Something hurt him then," he said aloud and pulled back on the line to see if he could turn the fish. But when he was touching the breaking point he held steady and settled back against the strain of the line.

"You're feeling it now, fish," he said. "And so, God knows, am I."

He looked around for the bird now because he would have liked him for company. The bird was gone.

You did not stay long, the man thought. But it is rougher where you are going until you make the shore. How did I let the fish cut me with that one quick pull he made? I must be getting very stupid. Or perhaps I was looking at the small bird and thinking of him. Now I will pay attention to my work and then I must eat the tuna so that I will not have a failure of strength.

harshness as he leaned back to pull and knew he could put no more strain on it. I must not jerk it ever, he thought. Each jerk widens the cut the hook makes and then when he does jump he might throw it. Anyway I feel better with the sun and for once I do not have to look into it.

There was yellow weed on the line but the old man knew that only made an added drag and he was pleased. It was the yellow Gulf weed that had made so much phosphorescence in the night.

"Fish," he said, "I love you and respect you very much. But I will kill you dead before this day ends."

Let us hope so, he thought.

A small bird came toward the skiff from the north. He was a warbler and flying very low over the water. The old man could see that he was very tired.

The bird made the stern of the boat and rested there. Then he flew around the old man's head and rested on the line where he was more comfortable.

"How old are you?" the old man asked the bird. "Is this your first trip?"

The bird looked at him when he spoke. He was too tired even to examine the line and he teetered on it as his delicate feet gripped it fast.

"It's steady," the old man told him. "It's too steady. You shouldn't be that tired after a windless night. What are birds coming to?"

The hawks, he thought, that come out to sea to meet them. But he said nothing of this to the bird who could not understand him anyway and who would learn about the hawks soon enough.

badly as mine does. But he cannot pull this skiff forever, no matter how great he is. Now everything is cleared away that might make trouble and I have a big reserve of line; all that a man can ask.

"Fish," he said softly, aloud, "I'll stay with you until I am dead."

He'll stay with me too, I suppose, the old man thought and he waited for it to be light. It was cold now in the time before daylight and he pushed against the wood to be warm. I can do it as long as he can, he thought. And in the first light the line extended out and down into the water. The boat moved steadily and when the first edge of the sun rose it was on the old man's right shoulder.

"He's headed north," the old man said. The current will have set us far to the eastward, he thought. I wish he would turn with the current. That would show that he was tiring.

When the sun had risen further the old man realized that the fish was not tiring. There was only one favorable sign. The slant of the line showed he was swimming at a lesser depth. That did not necessarily mean that he would jump. But he might.

"God let him jump," the old man said. "I have enough line to handle him."

Maybe if I can increase the tension just a little it will hurt him and he will jump, he thought. Now that it is daylight let him jump so that he'll fill the sacks along his backbone with air and then he cannot go deep to die.

He tried to increase the tension, but the line had been taut up to the very edge of the breaking point since he had hooked the fish and he felt the line closest to him and in the dark made the loose ends of the reserve coils fast. He worked skillfully with the one hand and put his foot on the coils to hold them as he drew his knots tight. Now he had six reserve coils of line. There were two from each bait he had severed and the two from the bait the fish had taken and they were all connected.

After it is light, he thought, I will work back to the forty-fathom bait and cut it away too and link up the reserve coils. I will have lost two hundred fathoms of good Catalan *cardel* and the hooks and leaders. That can be replaced. But who replaces this fish if I hook some fish and it cuts him off? I don't know what that fish was that took the bait just now. It could have been a marlin or a broadbill or a shark. I never felt him. I had to get rid of him too fast.

Aloud he said, "I wish I had the boy."

But you haven't got the boy, he thought. You have only yourself and you had better work back to the last line now, in the dark or not in the dark, and cut it away and hook up the two reserve coils.

So he did it. It was difficult in the dark and once the fish made a surge that pulled him down on his face and made a cut below his eye. The blood ran down his cheek a little way. But it coagulated and dried before it reached his chin and he worked his way back to the bow and rested against the wood. He adjusted the sack and carefully worked the line so that it came across a new part of his shoulders and, holding it anchored with his shoulders, he carefully felt the pull of the fish and then felt with his hand the progress of the skiff through the water.

I wonder what he made that lurch for, he thought. The wire must have slipped on the great hill of his back. Certainly his back cannot feel as

old man was clearing the lines and preparing the harpoon, the male fish jumped high into the air beside the boat to see where the female was and then went down deep, his lavender wings, that were his pectoral fins, spread wide and all his wide lavender stripes showing. He was beautiful, the old man remembered, and he had stayed.

That was the saddest thing I ever saw with them, the old man thought. The boy was sad too and we begged her pardon and butchered her promptly.

"I wish the boy was here," he said aloud and settled himself against the rounded planks of the bow and felt the strength of the great fish through the line he held across his shoulders moving steadily toward whatever he had chosen.

When once, through my treachery, it had been necessary to him to make a choice, the old man thought.

His choice had been to stay in the deep dark water far out beyond all snares and traps and treacheries. My choice was to go there to find him beyond all people. Beyond all people in the world. Now we are joined together and have been since noon. And no one to help either one of us.

Perhaps I should not have been a fisherman, he thought. But that was the thing that I was born for. I must surely remember to eat the tuna after it gets light.

Some time before daylight something took one of the baits that were behind him. He heard the stick break and the line begin to rush out over the gunwale of the skiff. In the darkness he loosened his sheath knife and taking all the strain of the fish on his left shoulder he leaned back and cut the line against the wood of the gunwale. Then he cut the other must eat him in the morning. Remember, he said to himself.

During the night two porpoises came around the boat and he could hear them rolling and blowing. He could tell the difference between the blowing noise the male made and the sighing blow of the female.

"They are good," he said. "They play and make jokes and love one another. They are our brothers like the flying fish."

Then he began to pity the great fish that he had hooked. He is wonderful and strange and who knows how old he is, he thought. Never have I had such a strong fish nor one who acted so strangely. Perhaps he is too wise to jump. He could ruin me by jumping or by a wild rush. But perhaps he has been hooked many times before and he knows that this is how he should make his fight. He cannot know that it is only one man against him, nor that it is an old man. But what a great fish he is and what will he bring in the market if the flesh is good. He took the bait like a male and he pulls like a male and his fight has no panic in it. I wonder if he has any plans or if he is just as desperate as I am?

He remembered the time he had hooked one of a pair of marlin. The male fish always let the female fish feed first and the hooked·fish, the female, made a wild, panic-stricken, despairing fight that soon exhausted her, and all the time the male had stayed with her, crossing the line and circling with her on the surface. He had stayed so close that the old man was afraid he would cut the line with his tail which was sharp as a scythe and almost of that size and shape. When the old man had gaffed her and clubbed her, holding the rapier bill with its sandpaper edge and clubbing her across the top of her head until her colour turned to a colour almost like the backing of mirrors, and then, with the boy's aid, hoisted her aboard, the male fish had stayed by the side of the boat. Then, while the

The fish never changed his course nor his direction all that night as far as the man could tell from watching the stars. It was cold after the sun went down and the old man's sweat dried cold on his back and his arms and his old legs. During the day he had taken the sack that covered the bait box and spread it in the sun to dry. After the sun went down he tied it around his neck so that it hung down over his back and he cautiously worked it down under the line that was across his shoulders now. The sack cushioned the line and he had found a way of leaning forward against the bow so that he was almost comfortable. The position actually was only somewhat less intolerable; but he thought of it as almost comfortable.

I can do nothing with him and he can do nothing with me, he thought. Not as long as he keeps this up.

Once he stood up and urinated over the side of the skiff and looked at the stars and checked his course. The line showed like a phosphorescent streak in the water straight out from his shoulders. They were moving more slowly now and the glow of Havana was not so strong, so that he knew the current must be carrying them to the eastward. If I lose the glare of Havana we must be going more to the eastward, he thought. For if the fish's course held true I must see it for many more hours. I wonder how the baseball came out in the grand leagues today, he thought. It would be wonderful to do this with a radio. Then he thought, think of it always. Think of what you are doing. You must do nothing stupid.

Then he said aloud, "I wish I had the boy. To help me and to see this."

No one should be alone in their old age, he thought. But it is unavoidable. I must remember to eat the tuna before he spoils in order to keep strong. Remember, no matter how little you want to, that you sounds and dies I don't know. But I'll do something. There are plenty of things I can do.

He held the line against his back and watched its slant in the water and the skiff moving steadily to the north-west.

This will kill him, the old man thought. He can't do this forever. But four hours later the fish was still swimming steadily out to sea, towing the skiff, and the old man was still braced solidly with the line across his back.

"It was noon when I hooked him," he said. "And I have never seen him."

He had pushed his straw hat hard down on his head before he hooked the fish and it was cutting his forehead. He was thirsty too and he got down on his knees and, being careful not to jerk on the line, moved as far into the bow as he could get and reached the water bottle with one hand. He opened it and drank a little. Then he rested against the bow. He rested sitting on the un-stepped mast and sail and tried not to think but only to endure.

Then he looked behind him and saw that no land was visible. That makes no difference, he thought. I can always come in on the glow from Havana. There are two more hours before the sun sets and maybe he will come up before that. If he doesn't maybe he will come up with the moon. If he does not do that maybe he will come up with the sunrise. I have no cramps and I feel strong. It is he that has the hook in his mouth. But what a fish to pull like that. He must have his mouth shut tight on the wire. I wish I could see him. I wish I could see him only once to know what I have against me.

of the two reserve coils of the next line. Now he was ready. He had three forty-fathom coils of line in reserve now, as well as the coil he was using.

"Eat it a little more," he said. "Eat it well."

Eat it so that the point of the hook goes into your heart and kills you, he thought. Come up easy and let me put the harpoon into you. All right. Are you ready? Have you been long enough at table?

"Now!" he said aloud and struck hard with both hands, gained a yard of line and then struck again and again, swinging with each arm alternately on the cord with all the strength of his arms and the pivoted weight of his body.

Nothing happened. The fish just moved away slowly and the old man could not raise him an inch. His line was strong and made for heavy fish and he held it against his hack until it was so taut that beads of water were jumping from it. Then it began to make a slow hissing sound in the water and he still held it, bracing himself against the thwart and leaning back against the pull. The boat began to move slowly off toward the north-west.

The fish moved steadily and they travelled slowly on the calm water. The other baits were still in the water but there was nothing to be done.

"I wish I had the boy" the old man said aloud. "I'm being towed by a fish and I'm the towing bitt. I could make the line fast. But then he could break it. I must hold him all I can and give him line when he must have it. Thank God he is travelling and not going down."

What I will do if he decides to go down, I don't know. What I'll do if he

He did not take it though. He was gone and the old man felt nothing.

"He can't have gone," he said. "Christ knows he can't have gone. He's making a turn. Maybe he has been hooked before and he remembers something of it."

Then he felt the gentle touch on the line and he was happy.

"It was only his turn," he said. "He'll take it."

He was happy feeling the gentle pulling and then he felt something hard and unbelievably heavy. It was the weight of the fish and he let the line slip down, down, down, unrolling off the first of the two reserve coils. As it went down, slipping lightly through the old man's fingers, he still could feel the great weight, though the pressure of his thumb and finger were almost imperceptible.

"What a fish," he said. "He has it sideways in his mouth now and he is moving off with it."

Then he will turn and swallow it, he thought. He did not say that because he knew that if you said a good thing it might not happen. He knew what a huge fish this was and he thought of him moving away in the darkness with the tuna held crosswise in his mouth. At that moment he felt him stop moving but the weight was still there. Then the weight increased and he gave more line. He tightened the pressure of his thumb and finger for a moment and the weight increased and was going straight down.

"He's taken it," he said. "Now I'll let him eat it well."

He let the line slip through his fingers while he reached down with his left hand and made fast the free end of the two reserve coils to the loop

"Yes," he said. "Yes," and shipped his oars without bumping the boat. He reached out for the line and held it softly between the thumb and forefinger of his right hand. He felt no strain nor weight and he held the line lightly. Then it came again. This time it was a tentative pull, not solid nor heavy, and he knew exactly what it was. One hundred fathoms down a marlin was eating the sardines that covered the point and the shank of the hook where the hand-forged hook projected from the head of the small tuna.

The old man held the line delicately, and softly, with his left hand, unleashed it from the stick. Now he could let it run through his fingers without the fish feeling any tension.

This far out, he must be huge in this month, he thought. Eat them, fish. Eat them. Please eat them. How fresh they are and you down there six hundred feet in that cold water in the dark. Make another turn in the dark and come back and eat them.

He felt the light delicate pulling and then a harder pull when a sardine's head must have been more difficult to break from the hook. Then there was nothing.

"Come on," the old man said aloud. "Make another turn. Just smell them. Aren't they lovely? Eat them good now and then there is the tuna. Hard and cold and lovely. Don't be shy, fish. Eat them."

He waited with the line between his thumb and his finger, watching it and the other lines at the same time for the fish might have swum up or down. Then came the same delicate pulling touch again.

"He'll take it," the old man said aloud. "God help him to take it."

the rich have radios to talk to them in their boats and to bring them the baseball."

Now is no time to think of baseball, he thought. Now is the time to think of only one thing. That which I was born for. There might be a big one around that school, he thought. I picked up only a straggler from the albacore that were feeding. But they are working far out and fast. Everything that shows on the surface today travels very fast and to the north-east. Can that be the time of day? Or is it some sign of weather that I do not know?

He could not see the green of the shore now but only the tops of the blue hills that showed white as though they were snow-capped and the clouds that looked like high snow mountains above them. The sea was very dark and the light made prisms in the water. The myriad flecks of the plankton were annulled now by the high sun and it was only the great deep prisms in the blue water that the old man saw now with his lines going straight down into the water that was a mile deep.

The tuna, the fishermen called all the fish of that species tuna and only distinguished among them by their proper names when they came to sell them or to trade them for baits, were down again. The sun was hot now and the old man felt it on the back of his neck and felt the sweat trickle down his back as he rowed.

I could just drift, he thought, and sleep and put a bight of line around my toe to wake me. But today is eighty-five days and I should fish the day well.

Just then, watching his lines, he saw one of the projecting green sticks dip sharply.

their panic.

"The bird is a great help," the old man said. Just then the stern line came taut under his foot, where he had kept a loop of the line, and he dropped his oars and felt the weight of the small tuna's shivering pull as he held the line firm and commenced to haul it in. The shivering increased as he pulled in and he could see the blue back of the fish in the water and the gold of his sides before he swung him over the side and into the boat. He lay in the stern in the sun, compact and bullet shaped, his big, unintelligent eyes staring as he thumped his life out against the planking of the boat with the quick shivering strokes of his neat, fast-moving tail. The old man hit him on the head for kindness and kicked him, his body still shuddering, under the shade of the stern.

"Albacore," he said aloud. "He'll make a beautiful bait. He'll weigh ten pounds."

He did not remember when he had first started to talk aloud when he was by himself. He had sung when he was by himself in the old days and he had sung at night sometimes when he was alone steering on his watch in the smacks or in the turtle boats. He had probably started to talk aloud, when alone, when the boy had left. But he did not remember. When he and the boy fished together they usually spoke only when it was necessary. They talked at night or when they were storm-bound by bad weather. It was considered a virtue not to talk unnecessarily at sea and the old man had always considered it so and respected it. But now he said his thoughts aloud many times since there was no one that they could annoy.

"If the others heard me talking out loud they would think that I am crazy," he said aloud. "But since I am not crazy, I do not care. And loggerheads, yellow in their armour-plating, strange in their love-making, and happily eating the Portuguese men-of-war with their eyes shut.

He had no mysticism about turtles although he had gone in turtle boats for many years. He was sorry for them all, even the great trunk backs that were as long as the skiff and weighed a ton. Most people are heartless about turtles because a turtle's heart will beat for hours after he has been cut up and butchered. But the old man thought, I have such a heart too and my feet and hands are like theirs. He ate the white eggs to give himself strength. He ate them all through May to be strong in September and October for the truly big fish.

He also drank a cup of shark liver oil each day from the big drum in the shack where many of the fishermen kept their gear. It was there for all fishermen who wanted it. Most fishermen hated the taste. But it was no worse than getting up at the hours that they rose and it was very good against all colds and grippes and it was good for the eyes.

Now the old man looked up and saw that the bird was circling again. "He's found fish," he said aloud. No flying fish broke the surface and there was no scattering of bait fish. But as the old man watched, a small tuna rose in the air, turned and dropped head first into the water. The tuna shone silver in the sun and after he had dropped back into the water another and another rose and they were jumping in all directions, churning the water and leaping in long jumps after the bait. They were circling it and driving it.

If they don't travel too fast I will get into them, the old man thought, and he watched the school working the water white and the bird now dropping and dipping into the bait fish that were forced to the surface in

that the sun was higher, meant good weather and so did the shape of the clouds over the land. But the bird was almost out of sight now and nothing showed on the surface of the water but some patches of yellow, sun-bleached Sargasso weed and the purple, formalized, iridescent, gelatinous bladder of a Portuguese man-of-war floating dose beside the boat. It turned on its side and then righted itself. It floated cheerfully as a bubble with its long deadly purple filaments trailing a yard behind it in the water.

"*Agua mala,*" the man said. "You whore."

From where he swung lightly against his oars he looked down into the water and saw the tiny fish that were coloured like the trailing filaments and swam between them and under the small shade the bubble made as it drifted. They were immune to its poison. But men were not and when same of the filaments would catch on a line and rest there slimy and purple while the old man was working a fish, he would have welts and sores on his arms and hands of the sort that poison ivy or poison oak can give. But these poisonings from the *agua mala* came quickly and struck like a whiplash.

The iridescent bubbles were beautiful. But they were the falsest thing in the sea and the old man loved to see the big sea turtles eating them. The turtles saw them, approached them from the front, then shut their eyes so they were completely carapaced and ate them filaments and all. The old man loved to see the turtles eat them and he loved to walk on them on the beach after a storm and hear them pop when he stepped on them with the horny soles of his feet.

He loved green turtles and hawk-bills with their elegance and speed and their great value and he had a friendly contempt for the huge, stupid

He shipped his oars and brought a small line from under the bow. It had a wire leader and a medium-sized hook and he baited it with one of the sardines. He let it go over the side and then made it fast to a ring bolt in the stern. Then he baited another line and left it coiled in the shade of the bow. He went back to rowing and to watching the long-winged black bird who was working, now, low over the water.

As he watched the bird dipped again slanting his wings for the dive and then swinging them wildly and ineffectually as he followed the flying fish. The old man could see the slight bulge in the water that the big dolphin raised as they followed the escaping fish. The dolphin were cutting through the water below the flight of the fish and would be in the water, driving at speed, when the fish dropped. It is a big school of dolphin, he thought. They are widespread and the flying fish have little chance. The bird has no chance. The flying fish are too big for him and they go too fast.

He watched the flying fish burst out again and again and the ineffectual movements of the bird. That school has gotten away from me, he thought. They are moving out too fast and too far. But perhaps I will pick up a stray and perhaps my big fish is around them. My big fish must be somewhere.

The clouds over the land now rose like mountains and the coast was only a long green line with the gray blue hills behind it. The water was a dark blue now, so dark that it was almost purple. As he looked down into it he saw the red sifting of the plankton in the dark water and the strange light the sun made now. He watched his lines to see them go straight down out of sight into the water and he was happy to see so much plankton because it meant fish. The strange light the sun made in the water, now

fishermen thought they were at a hundred.

But, he thought, I keep them with precision. Only I have no luck any more. But who knows? Maybe today. Every day is a new day. It is better to be lucky. But I would rather be exact. Then when luck comes you are ready.

The sun was two hours higher now and it did not hurt his eyes so much to look into the east. There were only three boats in sight now and they showed very low and far inshore.

All my life the early sun has hurt my eyes, he thought. Yet they are still good. In the evening I can look straight into it without getting the blackness. It has more force in the evening too. But in the morning it is painful.

Just then he saw a man-of-war bird with his long black wings circling in the sky ahead of him. He made a quick drop, slanting down on his back-swept wings, and then circled again.

"He's got something," the old man said aloud. "He's not just looking."

He rowed slowly and steadily toward where the bird was circling. He did not hurry and he kept his lines straight up and down. But he crowded the current a little so that he was still fishing correctly though faster than he would have fished if he was not trying to use the bird.

The bird went higher in the air and circled again, his wings motionless. Then he dove suddenly and the old man saw flying fish spurt out of the water and sail desperately over the surface.

"Dolphin," the old man said aloud. "Big dolphin."

with fresh sardines. Each sardine was hooked through both eyes so that they made a half-garland on the projecting steel. There was no part of the hook that a great fish could feel which was not sweet smelling and good tasting.

The boy had given him two fresh small tunas, or albacores, which hung on the two deepest lines like plummets and, on the others, he had a big blue runner and a yellow jack that had been used before; but they were in good condition still and had the excellent sardines to give them scent and attractiveness. Each line, as thick around as a big pencil, was looped onto a green-sapped stick so that any pull or touch on the bait would make the stick dip and each line had two forty-fathom coils which could be made fast to the other spare coils so that, if it were necessary, a fish could take out over three hundred fathoms of line.

Now the man watched the dip of the three sticks over the side of the skiff and rowed gently to keep the lines straight up and down and at their proper depths. It was quite light and any moment now the sun would rise.

The sun rose thinly from the sea and the old man could see the other boats, low on the water and well in toward the shore, spread out across the current. Then the sun was brighter and the glare came on the water and then, as it rose clear, the flat sea sent it back at his eyes so that it hurt sharply and he rowed without looking into it. He looked down into the water and watched the lines that went straight down into the dark of the water. He kept them straighter than anyone did, so that at each level in the darkness of the stream there would be a bait waiting exactly where he wished it to be for any fish that swam there. Others let them drift with the current and sometimes they were at sixty fathoms when the

She is kind and very beautiful. But she can be so cruel and it comes so suddenly and such birds that fly, dipping and hunting, with their small sad voices are made too delicately for the sea.

He always thought of the sea as *la mar* which is what people call her in Spanish when they love her. Sometimes those who love her say bad things of her but they are always said as though she were a woman. Some of the younger fishermen, those who used buoys as floats for their lines and had motorboats, bought when the shark livers had brought much money, spoke of her as *el mar* which is masculine. They spoke of her as a contestant or a place or even an enemy. But the old man always thought of her as feminine and as something that gave or withheld great favours, and if she did wild or wicked things it was because she could not help them. The moon affects her as it does a woman, he thought.

He was rowing steadily and it was no effort for him since he kept well within his speed and the surface of the ocean was flat except for the occasional swirls of the current. He was letting the current do a third of the work and as it started to be light he saw he was already further out than he had hoped to be at this hour.

I worked the deep wells for a week and did nothing, he thought. Today I'll work out where the schools of bonito and albacore are and maybe there will be a big one with them.

Before it was really light he had his baits out and was drifting with the current. One bait was down forty fathoms. The second was at seventy-five and the third and fourth were down in the blue water at one hundred and one hundred and twenty-five fathoms. Each bait hung head down with the shank of the hook inside the bait fish, tied and sewed solid and all the projecting part of the hook, the curve and the point, was covered onto the thole pins and, leaning forward against the thrust of the blades in the water, he began to row out of the harbour in the dark. There were other boats from the other beaches going out to sea and the old man heard the dip and push of their oars even though he could not see them now the moon was below the hills.

Sometimes someone would speak in a boat. But most of the boats were silent except for the dip of the oars. They spread apart after they were out of the mouth of the harbour and each one headed for the part of the ocean where he hoped to find fish. The old man knew he was going far out and he left the smell of the land behind and rowed out into the clean early morning smell of the ocean. He saw the phosphorescence of the Gulf weed in the water as he rowed over the part of the ocean that the fishermen called the great well because there was a sudden deep of seven hundred fathoms where all sorts of fish congregated because of the swirl the current made against the steep walls of the floor of the ocean. Here there were concentrations of shrimp and bait fish and sometimes schools of squid in the deepest holes and these rose close to the surface at night where all the wandering fish fed on them.

In the dark the old man could feel the morning coming and as he rowed he heard the trembling sound as flying fish left the water and the hissing that their stiff set wings made as they soared away in the darkness. He was very fond of flying fish as they were his principal friends on the ocean. He was sorry for the birds, especially the small delicate dark terns that were always flying and looking and almost never finding, and he thought, the birds have a harder life than we do except for the robber birds and the heavy strong ones. Why did they make birds so delicate and fine as those sea swallows when the ocean can be so cruel?

"We'll put the gear in the boat and then get some."

They had coffee from condensed milk cans at an early morning place that served fishermen.

"How did you sleep old man?" the boy asked. He was waking up now although it was still hard for him to leave his sleep.

"Very well, Manolin," the old man said. "I feel confident today."

"So do I," the boy said. "Now I must get your sardines and mine and your fresh baits. He brings our gear himself. He never wants anyone to carry anything."

"We're different," the old man said. "I let you carry things when you were five years old."

"I know it," the boy said. "I'll be right back. Have another coffee. We have credit here."

He walked off, bare-footed on the coral rocks, to the ice house where the baits were stored.

The old man drank his coffee slowly. It was all he would have all day and he knew that he should take it. For a long time now eating had bored him and he never carried a lunch. He had a bottle of water in the bow of the skiff and that was all he needed for the day.

The boy was back now with the sardines and the two baits wrapped in a newspaper and they went down the trail to the skiff, feeling the pebbled sand under their feet, and lifted the skiff and slid her into the water.

"Good luck old man."

"Good luck," the old man said. He fitted the rope lashings of the oars

his wife. He only dreamed of places now and of the lions on the beach.
They played like young cats in the dusk and he loved them as he loved
the boy. He never dreamed about the boy. He simply woke, looked out
the open door at the moon and unrolled his trousers and put them on. He
urinated outside the shack and then went up the road to wake the boy.
He was shivering with the morning cold. But he knew he would shiver
himself warm and that soon he would be rowing.

The door of the house where the boy lived was unlocked and he opened
it and walked in quietly with his bare feet. The boy was asleep on a cot
in the first room and the old man could see him clearly with the light that
came in from the dying moon. He took hold of one foot gently and held
it until the boy woke and turned and looked at him. The old man nodded
and the boy took his trousers from the chair by the bed and, sitting on
the bed, pulled them on.

The old man went out the door and the boy came after him. He was
sleepy and the old man put his arm across his shoulders and said, "I am
sorry."

"*Qué Va,*" the boy said. "It is what a man must do."

They walked down the road to the old man's shack and all along the
road, in the dark, barefoot men were moving, carrying the masts of their
boats.

When they reached the old man's shack the boy took the rolls of line in
the basket and the harpoon and gaff and the old man carried the mast
with the furled sail on his shoulder.

"Do you want coffee?" the boy asked.

"I don't know," the boy said. "All I know is that young boys sleep late and hard."

"I can remember it," the old man said. "I'll waken you in time."

"I do not like for him to waken me. It is as though I were inferior."

"I know."

"Sleep well old man."

The boy went out. They had eaten with no light on the table and the old man took off his trousers and went to bed in the dark. He rolled his trousers up to make a pillow, putting the newspaper inside them. He rolled himself in the blanket and slept on the other old newspapers that covered the springs of the bed.

He was asleep in a short time and he dreamed of Africa when he was a boy and the long golden beaches and the white beaches, so white they hurt your eyes, and the high capes and the great brown mountains. He lived along that coast now every night and in his dreams he heard the surf roar and saw the native boats come riding through it. He smelled the tar and oakum of the deck as he slept and he smelled the smell of Africa that the land breeze brought at morning.

Usually when he smelled the land breeze he woke up and dressed to go and wake the boy. But tonight the smell of the land breeze came very early and he knew it was too early in his dream and went on dreaming to see the white peaks of the Islands rising from the sea and then he dreamed of the different harbours and roadsteads of the Canary Islands.

He no longer dreamed of storms, nor of women, nor of great occurrences, nor of great fish, nor fights, nor contests of strength, nor of

"He was a great manager," the boy said. "My father thinks he was the greatest."

"Because he came here the most times," the old man said. "If Durocher had continued to come here each year your father would think him the greatest manager."

"Who is the greatest manager, really, Luque or Mike Gonzalez?"

"I think they are equal."

"And the best fisherman is you."

"No. I know others better."

"*Qué Va,*" the boy said. "There are many good fishermen and some great ones. But there is only you."

"Thank you. You make me happy. I hope no fish will come along so great that he will prove us wrong."

"There is no such fish if you are still strong as you say."

"I may not be as strong as I think," the old man said. "But I know many tricks and I have resolution."

"You ought to go to bed now so that you will be fresh in the morning. I will take the things back to the Terrace."

"Good night then. I will wake you in the morning."

"You're my alarm clock," the boy said.

"Age is my alarm clock," the old man said. "Why do old men wake so early? Is it to have one longer day?"

Dick Sisler and those great drives in the old park."

"There was nothing ever like them. He hits the longest ball I have ever seen."

"Do you remember when he used to come to the Terrace? I wanted to take him fishing but I was too timid to ask him. Then I asked you to ask him and you were too timid."

"I know. It was a great mistake. He might have gone with us. Then we would have that for all of our lives."

"I would like to take the great DiMaggio fishing," the old man said. "They say his father was a fisherman. Maybe he was as poor as we are and would understand."

"The great Sisler's father was never poor and he, the father, was playing in the Big Leagues when he was my age."

"When I was your age I was before the mast on a square rigged ship that ran to Africa and I have seen lions on the beaches in the evening."

"I know. You told me."

"Should we talk about Africa or about baseball?"

"Baseball I think," the boy said. "Tell me about the great John J. McGraw." He said *Jota* for J.

"He used to come to the Terrace sometimes too in the older days. But he was rough and harsh-spoken and difficult when he was drinking. His mind was on horses as well as baseball. At least he carried lists of horses at all times in his pocket and frequently spoke the names of horses on the telephone."

thoughtful for us."

"He sent two beers."

"I like the beer in cans best."

"I know. But this is in bottles, Hatuey beer, and I take back the bottles."

"That's very kind of you," the old man said. "Should we eat?"

"I've been asking you to," the boy told him gently. "I have not wished to open the container until you were ready."

"I'm ready now," the old man said. "I only needed time to wash."

Where did you wash? the boy thought. The village water supply was two streets down the road. I must have water here for him, the boy thought, and soap and a good towel. Why am I so thoughtless? I must get him another shirt and a jacket for the winter and some sort of shoes and another blanket.

"Your stew is excellent," the old man said.

"Tell me about the baseball," the boy asked him.

"In the American League it is the Yankees as I said," the old man said happily.

"They lost today," the boy told him.

"That means nothing. The great DiMaggio is himself again."

"They have other men on the team."

"Naturally. But he makes the difference. In the other league, between Brooklyn and Philadelphia I must take Brooklyn. But then I think of

"What have you got?" he asked.

"Supper," said the boy. "We're going to have supper."

"I'm not very hungry."

"Come on and eat. You can't fish and not eat."

"I have," the old man said getting up and taking the newspaper and folding it. Then he started to fold the blanket.

"Keep the blanket around you," the boy said. "You'll not fish without eating while I'm alive."

"Then live a long time and take care of yourself," the old man said. "What are we eating?"

"Black beans and rice, fried bananas, and some stew."

The boy had brought them in a two-decker metal container from the Terrace. The two sets of knives and forks and spoons were in his pocket with a paper napkin wrapped around each set.

"Who gave this to you?"

"Martin. The owner."

"I must thank him."

"I thanked him already," the boy said. "You don't need to thank him."

"I'll give him the belly meat of a big fish," the old man said. "Has he done this for us more than once?"

"I think so."

"I must give him something more than the belly meat then. He is very

"That's easy. I can always borrow two dollars and a half."

"I think perhaps I can too. But I try not to borrow. First you borrow. Then you beg."

"Keep warm old man," the boy said. "Remember we are in September."

"The month when the great fish come," the old man said. "Anyone can be a fisherman in May."

"I go now for the sardines," the boy said.

When the boy came back the old man was asleep in the chair and the sun was down. The boy took the old army blanket off the bed and spread it over the back of the chair and over the old man's shoulders. They were strange shoulders, still powerful although very old, and the neck was still strong too and the creases did not show so much when the old man was asleep and his head fallen forward. His shirt had been patched so many times that it was like the sail and the patches were faded to many different shades by the sun. The old man's head was very old though and with his eyes closed there was no life in his face. The newspaper lay across his knees and the weight of his arm held it there in the evening breeze. He was barefooted.

The boy left him there and when he came back the old man was still asleep.

"Wake up old man," the boy said and put his hand on one of the old man's knees.

The old man opened his eyes and for a moment he was coming back from a long way away. Then he smiled.

"Yes. I have yesterday's paper and I will read the baseball."

The boy did not know whether yesterday's paper was a fiction too. But the old man brought it out from under the bed.

"Pedrico gave it to me at the *bodega,*" he explained.

"I'll be back when I have the sardines. I'll keep yours and mine together on ice and we can share them in the morning. When I come back you can tell me about the baseball."

"The Yankees cannot lose."

"But I fear the Indians of Cleveland."

"Have faith in the Yankees my son. Think of the great DiMaggio."

"I fear both the Tigers of Detroit and the Indians of Cleveland."

"Be careful or you will fear even the Reds of Cincinnati and the White Sax of Chicago."

"You study it and tell me when I come back."

"Do you think we should buy a terminal of the lottery with an eighty-five? Tomorrow is the eighty-fifth day."

"We can do that," the boy said. "But what about the eighty-seven of your great record?"

"It could not happen twice. Do you think you can find an eighty-five?"

"I can order one."

"One sheet. That's two dollars and a half. Who can we borrow that from?"

through its open door. The old man leaned the mast with its wrapped sail against the wall and the boy put the box and the other gear beside it. The mast was nearly as long as the one room of the shack. The shack was made of the tough budshields of the royal palm which are called *guano* and in it there was a bed, a table, one chair, and a place on the dirt floor to cook with charcoal. On the brown walls of the flattened, overlapping leaves of the sturdy fibered *guano* there was a picture in color of the Sacred Heart of Jesus and another of the Virgin of Cobre. These were relics of his wife. Once there had been a tinted photograph of his wife on the wall but he had taken it down because it made him too lonely to see it and it was on the shelf in the corner under his clean shirt.

"What do you have to eat?" the boy asked.

"A pot of yellow rice with fish. Do you want some?"

"No. I will eat at home. Do you want me to make the fire?"

"No. I will make it later on. Or I may eat the rice cold."

"May I take the cast net?"

"Of course."

There was no cast net and the boy remembered when they had sold it. But they went through this fiction every day. There was no pot of yellow rice and fish and the boy knew this too.

"Eighty-five is a lucky number," the old man said. "How would you like to see me bring one in that dressed out over a thousand pounds?"

"I'll get the cast net and go for sardines. Will you sit in the sun in the doorway?"

"He does not like to work too far out."

"No," the boy said. "But I will see something that he cannot see such as a bird working and get him to come out after dolphin."

"Are his eyes that bad?"

"He is almost blind."

"It is strange," the old man said. "He never went turtle-ing. That is what kills the eyes."

"But you went turtle-ing for years off the Mosquito Coast and your eyes are good."

"I am a strange old man."

"But are you strong enough now for a truly big fish?"

"I think so. And there are many tricks."

"Let us take the stuff home," the boy said. "So I can get the cast net and go after the sardines."

They picked up the gear from the boat. The old man carried the mast on his shoulder and the boy carried the wooden box with the coiled, hard-braided brown lines, the gaff and the harpoon with its shaft. The box with the baits was under the stern of the skiff along with the club that was used to subdue the big fish when they were brought alongside. No one would steal from the old man but it was better to take the sail and the heavy lines home as the dew was bad for them and, though he was quite sure no local people would steal from him, the old man thought that a gaff and a harpoon were needless temptations to leave in a boat.

They walked up the road together to the old man's shack and went in

"Can you really remember that or did I just tell it to you?"

"I remember everything from when we first went together."

The old man looked at him with his sun-burned, confident loving eyes. "If you were my boy I'd take you out and gamble," he said. "But you are your father's and your mother's and you are in a lucky boat."

"May I get the sardines? I know where I can get four baits too."

"I have mine left from today. I put them in salt in the box."

"Let me get four fresh ones."

"One," the old man said. His hope and his confidence had never gone. But now they were freshening as when the breeze rises.

"Two," the boy said.

"Two," the old man agreed. "You didn't steal them?"

"I would," the boy said. "But I bought these."

"Thank you," the old man said. He was too simple to wonder when he had attained humility. But he knew he had attained it and he knew it was not disgraceful and it carried no loss of true pride.

"Tomorrow is going to be a good day with this current," he said.

"Where are you going?" the boy asked.

"Far out to come in when the wind shifts. I want to be out before it is light."

"I'll try to get him to work far out," the boy said. "Then if you hook something truly big we can come to your aid."

them to the shark factory on the other side of the cove where they were hoisted on a block and tackle, their livers removed, their fins cut off and their hides skinned out and their flesh cut into strips for salting.

When the wind was in the east a smell came across the harbour from the shark factory; but today there was only the faint edge of the odour because the wind had backed into the north and then dropped off and it was pleasant and sunny on the Terrace.

"Santiago," the boy said.

"Yes," the old man said. He was holding his glass and thinking of many years ago.

"Can I go out to get sardines for you for tomorrow?"

"No. Go and play baseball. I can still row and Rogelio will throw the net."

"I would like to go. If I cannot fish with you. I would like to serve in some way."

"You bought me a beer," the old man said. "You are already a man."

"How old was I when you first took me in a boat?"

"Five and you nearly were killed when I brought the fish in too green and he nearly tore the boat to pieces. Can you remember?"

"I can remember the tail slapping and banging and the thwart breaking and the noise of the clubbing. I can remember you throwing me into the bow where the wet coiled lines were and feeling the whole boat shiver and the noise of you clubbing him like chopping a tree down and the sweet blood smell all over me."

the skiff was hauled up. "I could go with you again. We've made some money."

The old man had taught the boy to fish and the boy loved him.

"No," the old man said. "You're with a lucky boat. Stay with them."

"But remember how you went eighty-seven days without fish and then we caught big ones every day for three weeks."

"I remember," the old man said. "I know you did not leave me because you doubted."

"It was papa made me leave. I am a boy and I must obey him."

"I know," the old man said. "It is quite normal."

"He hasn't much faith."

"No," the old man said. "But we have. Haven't we?"

"Yes," the boy said. "Can I offer you a beer on the Terrace and then we'll take the stuff home."

"Why not?" the old man said. "Between fishermen."

They sat on the Terrace and many of the fishermen made fun of the old man and he was not angry. Others, of the older fishermen, looked at him and were sad. But they did not show it and they spoke politely about the current and the depths they had drifted their lines at and the steady good weather and of what they had seen. The successful fishermen of that day were already in and had butchered their marlin out and carried them laid full length across two planks, with two men staggering at the end of each plank, to the fish house where they waited for the ice truck to carry them to the market in Havana. Those who had caught sharks had taken

THE OLD MAN
AND THE SEA

He was an old man who fished alone in a skiff in the Gulf Stream and he had gone eighty-four days now without taking a fish. In the first forty days a boy had been with him. But after forty days without a fish the boy's parents had told him that the old man was now definitely and finally *salao,* which is the worst form of unlucky, and the boy had gone at their orders in another boat which caught three good fish the first week. It made the boy sad to see the old man come in each day with his skiff empty and he always went down to help him carry either the coiled lines or the gaff and harpoon and the sail that was furled around the mast. The sail was patched with flour sacks and, furled, it looked like the flag of permanent defeat.

The old man was thin and gaunt with deep wrinkles in the back of his neck. The brown blotches of the benevolent skin cancer the sun brings from its reflection on the tropic sea were on his cheeks. The blotches ran well down the sides of his face and his hands had the deep-creased scars from handling heavy fish on the cords. But none of these scars were fresh. They were as old as erosions in a fishless desert.

Everything about him was old except his eyes and they were the same color as the sea and were cheerful and undefeated.

"Santiago," the boy said to him as they climbed the bank from where

THE
OLD MAN
AND
THE SEA

老人與海 / 歐內斯特 . 海明威著；魯羊譯 . -- 初版 . -- 臺北市：時報文化，2019.08

面； 公分 . -- （愛經典；22）

譯自：The old man and the sea

ISBN 978-957-13-7907-4（精裝）

874.59 108012242

本書根據海明威 1952 年授權的紐約 CHARLES SCRIBNER'S SONS 經典版本譯出

作家榜经典文库®
★ ★ ★ ★ ★ ★ ★ ★ ★ ★ ★

ISBN 978-957-13-7907-4

Printed in Taiwan

愛經典 0 0 2 2

老人與海

作者一歐內斯特・海明威｜譯者一魯羊｜編輯總監一蘇清霖｜編輯一邱淑鈴｜美術設計一FE 設計
｜封面繪圖（老人）一邵飛｜內頁繪圖一Slava Shults｜校對一邱淑鈴｜董事長一趙政岷｜出版者一時報文化
出版企業股份有限公司　108019 台北市和平西路三段二四〇號四樓　發行專線一（〇二）二三〇六一六八四二
讀者服務專線一〇八〇〇一二三一一七〇五、（〇二）二三〇四一七一〇三　讀者服務傳真一（〇二）二三〇
四一六八五八　郵撥一一九三四四七二四時報文化出版公司　信箱一一〇八九九臺北華江橋郵局第九九信箱　時
報悅讀網一http://www.readingtimes.com.tw｜電子郵件信箱 new@readingtimes.com.tw｜法律顧問一理律法
律事務所　陳長文律師、李念祖律師｜印刷一勁達印刷有限公司｜初版一刷一二〇一九年八月十六日｜初版
十三刷一二〇二三年十月五日｜定價一新台幣三五〇元｜版權所有　翻印必究（缺頁或破損的書，請寄回更
換）

時報文化出版公司成立於一九七五年，並於一九九九年股票上櫃公開發行，於二〇〇八年脫離中時
集團非屬旺中，以「尊重智慧與創意的文化事業」為信念。